Charm Hall

P
N

1   The Magic Begins
2   Midnight Mayhem
3   Toil and Trouble
4   Mona Lisa Mystery

AND COMING SOON

5   A Note of Danger
6   Mirror Magic

Charm Hall

Toil and Trouble

Tabitha Black

h

**Hodder
Children's
Books**

A division of Hachette Children's Books

Special thanks to Narinder Dhami

Copyright © 2007 Working Partners Ltd
Created by Working Partners Limited, London, WC1X 9HH
Illustrations copyright © 2007 Margaret Chamberlain

First published in Great Britain in 2007 by Hodder Children's Books

The rights of Tabitha Black and Margaret Chamberlain to
be identified as the Author and Illustrator of the Work respectively
have been asserted by them in accordance with the
Copyright, Designs and Patents Act 1988

1

A Catalogue record for this book is available from the British Library

ISBN 978 0 340 93142 4

Typeset in Weiss by Avon DataSet Ltd,
Bidford on Avon, Warwickshire

Printed in Great Britain by
Clays Ltd, St Ives plc

The paper and board used in this paperback by Hodder Children's
Books are natural recyclable products made from wood grown in
sustainable forests. The manufacturing processes conform to the
environmental regulations of the country of origin.

Hodder Children's Books
a division of Hachette Children's Books
338 Euston Road, London NW1 3BH
An Hachette Livre UK company

Chapter One

"Hello, everyone! I'm back!"

Paige Hart burst into her dorm room at Charm Hall Boarding School, her auburn hair flying, and a huge grin on her face. She'd been looking forward to this moment ever since she'd said goodbye to her mum and dad at the airport in Dubai.

Shannon Carroll and Summer Kirby, Paige's best friends, were standing by their beds unpacking their suitcases. But when they saw Paige, they both dropped the piles of clothes they were holding and dashed across the room, yelling out a greeting.

"Oh, Paige, it's great to see you!" Shannon

declared, grabbing her friend in a bearhug. "Did you have a good time in Dubai?"

"Ooh, you're so brown, Paige!" Summer laughed. "I'm *really* jealous."

Paige grinned. "Dubai was great, but it's brilliant to be back!" she exclaimed.

It was hard for Paige to believe that, last term, when her dad had suddenly been sent to Dubai for his work, she hadn't wanted to come to Charm Hall. Today, when Paige had arrived back at the beautiful old manor house again, it had felt just like coming home. "Where's Velvet?" she asked eagerly.

As she spoke, Paige felt something furry brush against her legs, and she looked down to see the small jet-black kitten at her feet. Velvet was purring loudly and staring up at Paige with her warm golden eyes.

"Hello, Velvet!" Paige said, sweeping the kitten up into her arms. "I've missed you!"

Velvet purred even louder, and pushed her nose against Paige's cheek.

"I know you liked Dubai, but I bet you didn't meet any magical kittens, like Velvet, out there!" Shannon teased.

2

Paige laughed. The three girls had found out about Velvet's magical powers during the previous term. The kitten had arrived in their dorm room one stormy afternoon, and Paige, Summer and Shannon had soon realized that Velvet was no ordinary cat.

"I'd better start unpacking," Paige said, putting Velvet gently down on the floor. Her suitcase had been sent on ahead and was already lying on her bed. "I've got presents for you all from Dubai!"

"Ooh, I love presents!" gasped Shannon.

Velvet leaped up on to Paige's bed and sniffed curiously at the suitcase as Paige threw back the lid.

"These are for you!" Paige told her friends, holding out two giftbags.

Shannon and Summer took the bags and peered inside. They both grinned at Paige when they saw the silver bangles she'd brought them.

"Thanks, Paige!" they said together.

"I got some sweets for Joan as well," Paige added. "To thank her for feeding Velvet while we were away.' Joan was one of the school dinner ladies. She had seen Velvet around the school grounds and assumed that the kitten was from a nearby farm.

She knew the girls fed Velvet and so she had offered to carry on doing so while the girls were away over the summer. Joan didn't know Velvet lived in the girls' dorm though. That was a big secret, because pets weren't allowed at Charm Hall.

Meanwhile, Velvet had jumped into Paige's suitcase and was padding around on top of the clothes, sniffing curiously.

"Yes, I've got something for you, too, Velvet!" Paige laughed. She rooted around in the case and held up a pink mouse attached to a long golden string. Velvet fixed the mouse with an intent gaze, and then leaped at it as Paige swung it above her head.

"Velvet's getting a bit spoiled!" Shannon remarked, shaking her head as Velvet continued to bat the mouse to and fro. "She's got so many toys! Summer's brought her a little ball with a bell inside."

"And what about *you*?" Summer demanded, laughing. "*You* bought her a box of treats!"

Shannon grinned and glanced at Velvet, who, having just knocked her mouse to the floor, was getting ready to pounce. "Well, the supermarket at home had a much bigger selection than the shop at

the end of the school drive," she said. "And Velvet's mad about her treats!"

Paige began unpacking, and Summer and Shannon went back to their own suitcases.

"Oh, I've brought this too.' Shannon held up a silver torch and waved it in the air. "Now we'll be able to see what we're eating when we have our midnight feasts!"

"Great idea, Shannon," agreed Summer. "My phone torch didn't give us enough light. Do you remember when I dropped that big bag of crisps and they went all over the floor? We were crawling around for ages, trying to see to pick them all up!"

Paige and Shannon laughed.

"Well, we'll have a *fantastic* midnight feast tonight," said Shannon, waving some chocolate bars.

Paige heaved a happy sigh. A new term at Charm Hall was starting and she had a feeling it was going to be just as much fun as the last.

"You know what you were saying yesterday, about how great it is to be back at Charm Hall?" Shannon whispered to Paige the next morning after breakfast. The girls were on their way to a special assembly to welcome everyone back to school.

Paige nodded, looking puzzled.

"Well," Shannon went on in a low voice, "not even Charm Hall's perfect!" And she nodded at the group of girls in front of them.

"Oh, I'm *so* glad we didn't go to boring old Spain!" Abigail Carter was saying to her dorm-mates, Mia and Chloe. "My parents took me to Florida for two weeks, and we stayed in a *really* posh hotel."

Paige pulled a face at Shannon and Summer. Abigail Carter was in their form, and she was a *major* pain.

"I'd forgotten all about Abigail," Paige said with a grin.

"Lucky you!" Summer winked at her.

The girls entered the hall and Paige looked round at the high, arched windows and the wood-panelled walls.

Then Shannon nudged her. "Check out the newbie teacher," she whispered to Paige and Summer. "Just behind Miss Collins."

Paige tried to glance over her shoulder without being too obvious. There was a woman she'd never seen before sitting just behind their English teacher. She had black hair drawn back off her face, and green eyes.

"Maybe she's our new history teacher," Summer suggested. "Miss Gordon left at the end of last term."

But the girls didn't have time to speculate any more as Miss Linnet, the headmistress, swept into the hall at that very moment. Silence fell as she mounted the stage.

"Welcome back, girls!" Miss Linnet began with a smile. "I can't tell you how pleased I am to see you all here for the new term at Charm Hall. I am *especially* pleased after the events of last term!"

Paige glanced at Summer and Shannon. The school had been on the verge of closing, due to part of Lavinia Charm's will being lost. The vital piece of paper which meant that the school could stay open had finally been found because of Velvet.

"Before we begin, I would like to welcome two new members of staff," Miss Linnet went on. "We have a new caretaker, Sam Morris, whom I'm sure you will see around the grounds."

Everyone, including Paige, Summer and Shannon, looked round to see a middle-aged man with grey-streaked dark hair and steady brown eyes sitting at the back of the hall.

"We also have a new history teacher," Miss Linnet continued. "Mrs Stockbridge." The head smiled at the woman the three friends had been looking at. "I know you'll both enjoy your time here."

"I wonder what Mrs Stockbridge is like," Shannon whispered to Paige.

Paige was about to reply when she saw Miss

Collins staring crossly at them, so she kept quiet.

"A new school year is always a wonderful time," Miss Linnet said. "It's the beginning of new adventures and new challenges. And this year, I would like to start things off with a bang!" She paused and looked around the hall. Everyone was hanging on the head's every word.

"And so," Miss Linnet continued, "I'm very pleased to tell you that we are going to have a big Hallowe'en party at the end of October!"

Chapter Two

There was a ripple of excitement through the hall as everyone began talking at once.

"A Hallowe'en party!" Paige exclaimed. "Do you think we'll be allowed to dress up?"

"Course we will!" declared Shannon. "Hallowe'en's just not Hallowe'en without loads of fake blood!"

Miss Linnet had given the pupils a few moments to talk, but now she raised her hand for silence. Gradually everyone quietened down.

"I'm going to need a committee to help with the party plans and decorations," she explained. "I shall be looking for volunteers from each year and from all four of the school houses. And, of course, we want you all to dress up!" Miss Linnet announced, her eyes twinkling as everyone in the hall started buzzing with excitement again. "There'll be a prize of two cinema tickets for the best costume."

"Let's volunteer for the committee!" Paige suggested eagerly.

Shannon nodded, but Summer frowned.

"I don't think I can," she said. "I'm going to be really busy practising my gymnastics this term."

"OK," Shannon agreed. "Looks like it's just you and me then, Paige."

"And we all have to decide what our costumes are going to be," said Paige.

"The more gruesome the better!" Summer said with a grin.

"Girls!" Miss Linnet held up her hand again. "If anyone is interested in volunteering for the committee, there's a list on the noticeboard outside the school office. So please sign up."

After assembly was over, the three friends went straight to the office so that Paige and Shannon could put their names down. There was already a queue.

"Look who's at the front," whispered Summer.

Abigail Carter was writing her name at the head of the list in very large letters. She signed off with a flourish and then, as she turned away, she caught sight of Paige, Shannon and Summer. Abigail tossed her hair over her shoulder arrogantly as she walked past. "What are you bothering to sign up for?" she asked coldly. "*You* won't get on the committee. Miss Linnet is looking for people with brains!"

"So why are you applying then?" Shannon asked.

Abigail glared at her. "Miss Linnet's bound to choose me!" she said fiercely.

"Well, we won't be *that* upset if we don't get picked," Shannon said breezily, "because it will just give us more time to work on our costumes. We have a really *brilliant* idea!"

"Oh!" Abigail looked slightly flustered. "Well . . . er . . . actually, so do I! You won't believe your eyes when you see *my* Hallowe'en costume!"

"It won't be as good as ours," Shannon said confidently.

Abigail looked thoroughly annoyed. "Maybe you shouldn't bother dressing up. Just go to the

12

Hallowe'en party as yourselves," she snapped tartly. "You're gruesome enough!" And she stalked off down the corridor, her nose in the air.

"Well!" Shannon said, shaking her head. "And what are you two staring at?" she added, as she turned to see Summer and Paige both looking eagerly at her.

"What's this brilliant idea for our costumes then?" Paige asked, and Summer nodded.

Shannon shrugged. "Haven't a clue!" she replied. "I just wanted to wind Abigail up."

Paige and Summer both groaned.

"I really believed you, Shannon!" Summer grumbled.

"Me too," Paige agreed. "You've really dropped us in it now! You *do* realize that we've got to think of some really fantastic costumes now, so we can win the prize *and* annoy Abigail!"

"I know," Shannon grinned. "We'd better put our thinking caps on!"

"It's nearly dinner time," Paige said, flinging her pen down on her desk as she finally finished her English homework. She turned to look at Shannon and

Summer, who were both still bent over their books. "Let's go and eat. I'm starving!"

It was a few days later. The school was still buzzing about the Hallowe'en party and Paige and Shannon were both delighted to have been chosen for Miss Linnet's decorating committee.

"I'm ready," Summer said. "How are you doing, Shannon?"

"I'm only halfway through this maths homework," Shannon groaned. "It's driving me crazy!" She glanced at Velvet who was stretched out on Summer's bed. "I bet you're glad you don't have to do long division, Velvet. Hey, maybe you could magically finish it off for me while I'm eating my dinner!"

Velvet opened one eye lazily, and gave Shannon a meaningful look, as if to say "you should know better", and then fell fast asleep again.

"I think that's definitely a 'no', Shannon," Paige laughed.

The girls left Velvet in their dorm and hurried down the stairs towards the dining hall.

"What are we going to do this evening after your committee meeting?" asked Summer. "Shall we go

14

to the JCR and play table tennis?"

"Sounds good," Shannon agreed. "I just hope Abigail isn't *too* annoying at the meeting," she added. "Why did Miss Linnet have to choose her to be on the committee as well?"

"I suppose Abigail is quite good at organizing stuff," Paige said grudgingly, as they neared the dining hall.

Just as they turned a corner in the corridor, Paige noticed that one of her shoelaces had come untied. She bent over to retie it, but as she did so someone cannoned into the back of her, almost knocking her over.

"What a stupid place to stop!" snapped Abigail crossly, sweeping past Paige and hurrying off.

"Typical Abigail!" Shannon said, shaking her head. "She bumped into you, and then she blames you for getting in her way!"

As the girls neared the dining hall, Paige noticed Abigail standing in the corridor, reading the messages pinned to the games noticeboard. She was very surprised when she saw Abigail sign up for a trip to the swimming pool in the nearby town.

Paige frowned, puzzled. She, Shannon and

Summer had signed up for the trip the day before, but everyone knew that Abigail *hated* swimming.

"Weird!" Paige muttered to herself as she went into the dining hall. They simply couldn't get away from Abigail at the moment. At lunchtime, Abigail had deliberately chosen to sit next to them, then she'd bumped into Paige in the corridor, and now she was coming on the swimming trip with them.

Paige shook her head in bewilderment. They'd only been back at school for four days and already things were getting weird. What was Abigail up to?

"Look at all the leaves," Paige remarked, gazing out at the school grounds as she, Shannon and Summer hurried along the corridor to their next lesson. It was now some weeks after the beginning of term, and autumn was really beginning to take hold. Paige and Shannon had already attended several committee meetings about the Hallowe'en party.

"At least Velvet's enjoying herself!" Summer laughed, pointing at the kitten who was chasing a gold leaf across the grass.

"I wonder what we'll be doing in history today,"

Paige mused as they reached the classroom. "I really like Mrs Stockbridge, don't you?"

"Yes, she's much nicer than Mrs Stark and her horrible maths!" Shannon agreed.

Paige nodded. Mrs Stockbridge seemed to have plenty of ideas for making their history lessons fun and exciting. They had just finished researching their family trees.

The girls went into the classroom and sat down in their usual places to wait for the teacher. Abigail dashed in a moment later. But instead of going to her usual seat next to her roommate, Mia, she sat down behind Shannon, Summer and Paige.

"Our shadow's back again!" Shannon whispered to Paige and Summer.

Paige frowned. Abigail seemed to have been following them everywhere for the last few weeks. Every time the girls turned around, there she was. Abigail had sat right behind them in the coach on the swimming trip, and she was always trying to get seats near them in lessons. But the girls had no idea what Abigail was playing at.

"Abigail, you're sitting in my place!" Melanie

Adams said as she arrived for the class. She was the one who usually sat behind the three friends.

"I don't see your name on it!" Abigail snapped. "And I got here first anyway."

Curiously Paige glanced round as Melanie shrugged and went off to sit somewhere else. *Why was Abigail so keen to sit behind them?*

At that moment Mrs Stockbridge came in. "Everyone in their seats, please," she said with a smile, putting a pile of papers on her desk. "Now I have a very exciting new project for you today, and I'd like you to split into small groups of three. Please move your chairs to different parts of the room if you have to."

"Well, that's easy!" Shannon grinned at Paige and Summer. "We don't even have to move!"

Paige glanced round to see what Abigail would do. Whenever they split into groups, Abigail always worked with Mia and Chloe, but they were sitting on the other side of the room.

Paige saw that Abigail was reluctantly picking up her chair and preparing to move. But as she did so, she looked disappointedly at Paige and her friends. Paige frowned as a really strange idea occurred to her. Could Abigail be shadowing them because she wanted to be *friends*?

"Good, now let's get started," Mrs Stockbridge said, interrupting Paige's thoughts. "Our work for the next few weeks is going to be based on the topic of Hallowe'en, which ties in rather nicely with the party you're all so excited about!"

There was a murmur of interest.

"I would like each group to choose a historical project based on Hallowe'en," Mrs Stockbridge went on. "You could look at how Hallowe'en celebrations have changed through the ages, for example. Or you could trace the history of witches and witch-finding in Britain, or you could do a project on any place that's said to be haunted, such as the Tower of London. In fact," she paused for a moment, "you could even do a project on Charm Hall itself. As some of you probably know, there's a rumour that some of the women in the Charm family were actually witches, and it might be interesting to follow that up."

Paige glanced immediately at Summer and Shannon. She knew *exactly* which project she wanted to choose!

"I shall give you the rest of the lesson to discuss with your group members which project you would like to do," Mrs Stockbridge finished.

Paige turned to her friends. "Shall we—"

"YES!" Summer and Shannon chorused eagerly.

"You don't even know what I'm going to say!" Paige laughed.

"You're going to say, 'let's do a project about Charm Hall'," Summer told her confidently.

"So that we can find out all about the Charm family," Shannon added with a grin. "And that kitten, in Lavinia Charm's portrait, who looks just like Velvet!"

Chapter Three

"OK, so where shall we start?" Paige asked, picking up her pen.

"Let's start by trying to find out a bit more about the history of the manor house," suggested Summer. "I bet there'll be something on the Internet."

"Good thinking!" said Shannon.

Mrs Stockbridge was making her way from group to group, discussing their choice of project. When she finally arrived at Paige, Shannon and Summer's table, she smiled at the long list of notes on Shannon's notepad.

"You seem to have a lot of ideas, girls," she

remarked. "Which project have you chosen?"

"We're going to do the history of Charm Hall," Shannon explained. "Just like you suggested."

Mrs Stockbridge nodded. "That sounds fascinating!"

"We thought we'd start by looking on the Internet," said Summer.

"Well, you have my permission to use the computer room during homework period and later this evening outside of the set times, too, if you wish," Mrs Stockbridge replied. "And do let me know if you uncover any particularly interesting information! I'll look forward to seeing your finished project, girls."

Paige found it quite difficult to concentrate on her other lessons for the rest of the day. She was so excited about their project and the chance to find out more about Velvet, she could hardly think about anything else.

The girls finished their other homework during study period, and then went down to dinner. After they'd eaten, they went straight to the computer room which, because it was now out of hours, was empty.

"I'm surprised Abigail isn't following us," Shannon remarked, pulling a chair up to the desk.

"Oh, Abigail, Mia and Chloe have gone off to start their project," Summer replied, switching on the computer.

"She sat behind us in science and again during dinner, though," added Paige, also pulling up a chair. "Abigail's hanging around so much, I'm beginning to wonder if she wants to be friends with us!"

"You *are* joking, aren't you, Paige?" Shannon said doubtfully. "I can't believe that's the reason!"

Summer began by entering a few phrases about Charm Hall in the search engine. The girls looked through the results, but most of the sites were mentioning the present-day school. A few links down, though, they found one which looked more interesting.

This website featured old and interesting houses throughout the UK, and Summer quickly scrolled through the index to find Charm Hall.

"Here we are," she said and began to read aloud. "'Charm Hall was built in medieval times. Over the years, parts of the house have been rebuilt, and now the majority of the existing building is Tudor.'"

"Look at the next bit," Paige said, pointing at the screen.

Summer read, "'Charm Hall is a fine example of a Tudor manor, having been unaffected by events which damaged lots of other historical buildings around the country. These include the Second World War and various major storms and floods.'"

"Charm Hall's obviously a lucky place!" Shannon laughed as they came to the end of the page.

They returned to the results that the search engine had thrown up and carried on working their way through the links.

"This site looks interesting," Summer said, clicking on the link. "It's about the history of witches in Britain."

The site was huge, with lots of different pages, but it had a long section entitled "The Charm Hall Witches".

"Look, it says that there's a popular myth that the women in the Charm family were witches," Shannon said, following the writing on the screen with her finger. "'This rumour probably began in the 1700s because of Estelle Charm, who was the daughter of Sir William, the sixth Lord Charm,'" Shannon read. " 'Estelle was the seventh daughter of a seventh daughter and, in more superstitious times, it was believed that the circumstances of her birth would give her certain magical powers.'"

"The seventh daughter of a seventh daughter?" Paige repeated, looking a bit confused.

"Sir William and his wife must have had six daughters already, and then they had Estelle," Summer said slowly.

"And Estelle's mum was born after *her* parents had already had six daughters, so she was a seventh daughter too," Shannon added.

"I wonder if Estelle was really a witch," Paige said thoughtfully.

"Let's try to find out!" Summer replied, glancing at the clock on the wall. "We've still got some time before bed, but we'd better hurry."

Quickly Paige typed 'Estelle Charm' and 'witch' into the search engine and began exploring the links. However, she was disappointed to find that there was very little extra information about Estelle on any of the sites.

Then Paige noticed the very last link on the page. " 'Famous Mysteries,' " she read. " 'The Charm family and the Eye of Heaven.' "

"The Eye of Heaven?" Shannon repeated, puzzled, as Paige went to the site. "What's that?"

" 'The Eye of Heaven is the name of a beautiful and flawless sapphire which once belonged to the Charm family,' " Paige read aloud. " 'There are many legends associated with this fabulous jewel. It was even said that the sapphire had been created by the gods and sent from heaven. However, scholars believe that it was originally brought over from India, since William, the sixth Lord Charm, travelled extensively in Asia.' "

"William was Estelle's father, wasn't he?" asked Shannon.

Paige nodded.

"So where's the Eye of Heaven now?" asked Summer.

" 'One of the largest and finest sapphires ever to have existed, the Eye of Heaven is therefore priceless – and yet it has not been seen for over two hundred years,' " Paige went on. " 'The stone was set in a magnificent golden necklace, and was last seen in the possession of the Charm family in the late 1700s . . .'"

"This is great stuff for our project!" Shannon said enthusiastically. "We can put in a section about the Eye of Heaven."

Paige nodded. "I wish we could find out more about Estelle, though," she sighed. "I'll try a different search engine."

Shannon and Summer watched as Paige patiently tried to bring up some sites with information that they hadn't already seen. But all she could find were some old news reports about Charm Hall School having been broken into several years ago.

Miaow!

All three girls jumped and looked round to see Velvet, standing in the doorway, staring quizzically at them with her slanting golden eyes.

"Hi, Velvet," said Shannon as the kitten padded lightly into the room. "Have you come to tell us it's time for bed?" She glanced at the clock again and let out a whistle. "It is nearly, too. We'd better go."

"I'll close this down," Paige said with a yawn, reaching for the mouse.

At just that moment, though, Velvet leaped up on to the desk and, before the girls could stop her, she walked right across the middle of the keyboard.

"Oh!" Paige jerked backwards in surprise as the screen flickered, and golden sparks seemed to fly from the monitor. "Velvet, what have you done?"

"Has she broken the computer?" Shannon asked, looking worried.

"No," Summer breathed, her eyes fixed on the screen. "Look!"

A new website had popped up. A virtual girl dressed in a long, old-fashioned pink and white dress was on the screen in front of them.

"Listen well, my friends," she said, staring straight at Paige, Shannon and Summer, "and I will tell you the true story of Estelle Charm and the Eye of Heaven."

The three friends huddled around the computer, hanging on the virtual girl's every word. Meanwhile, Velvet sat on the edge of the desk, swinging her tail slowly from side to side.

"Sir William, the sixth Lord Charm, and his wife, Margaret, had seven daughters," the girl went on. "Their names were Maria, Eliza, Sarah, Hannah,

Clarissa, Rebeckah and Estelle. Their eighth child was a boy called James."

As the girl named the Charm children, pictures of each one began to flash up on the screen, one after another. Estelle was dark-haired and pretty, with smiling brown eyes.

"Wait a minute," said Summer in a dazed voice. "Where have these pictures come from?"

"From this website, of course!" Shannon replied impatiently.

"No, I mean, these pictures aren't *paintings*," Summer explained. "They're more like photos," she frowned in bewilderment, "but there were no cameras in the late 1700s!"

Shannon and Paige glanced at each other in shock as they realized that Summer was right.

"You know what?" Summer went on, glancing at Velvet, perched on the edge of the desk. "I don't think this is an *ordinary* website at all. I think it's magic – Velvet's magic!"

Chapter Four

Paige nodded in agreement. Then, her heart pounding with excitement, she turned back to the website.

"Sadly, the eight Charm children lost their mother and father when they were still quite young," the virtual girl explained. "They died of a mysterious illness while they were on their travels. Estelle herself grew up to become skilled in the art of healing, and many of the people from the village around Charm Hall would come to her for help when they were ill."

"Oh, Estelle sounds cool!" Shannon said admiringly.

"Estelle could often cure the villagers with her potions," the girl went on. "She kept the details of her remedies in her journal, and so the rumour began that she was a witch. Many people in the village suspected that Estelle wrote spells in her journal, because she was never without it. And, besides, she was the seventh daughter of a seventh daughter . . ."

"*Was* she a witch?" Paige whispered.

The virtual girl looked straight at Paige. "She was indeed a witch," she went on, as if she was answering Paige directly. "Estelle had magical powers!"

Paige, Shannon and Summer gasped in amazement, electrified by what they'd just heard.

The girl on screen smiled and clicked her fingers. Immediately she disappeared from the computer screen to be replaced by what looked like a video clip. Trees swayed in a gale-force wind beneath dark, stormy skies.

"This is just like a film!" Paige cried.

"It is a very special night," said the virtual girl's voice. "Eliza Charm, Estelle's second sister, is to be married and tonight is her engagement ball."

Suddenly the scene changed as the camera seemed to zoom in on a trail of people walking towards a large building. Thunder crashed overhead, and lightning zigzagged across the dark sky, lighting up the front of the house.

"That's Charm Hall!" Shannon pointed out.

"Who are all those people?" Summer wanted to know. "Are they going to Eliza's engagement ball?"

The three girls watched the man at the front of the crowd bang on the door. They could hear music and laughter coming from inside the house, and the man had to hammer hard to make himself heard.

Suddenly the door opened. A pretty girl in a long red dress, her dark hair piled on top of her head, was standing in the entrance hall, looking out enquiringly.

"It's Estelle!" Summer exclaimed.

"Please, miss," the man who had banged on the door said, wringing his hands anxiously. "Will you help us!"

"I will, John Miller, if I can," said Estelle kindly, her dark eyes flicking over the crowd. "What is the matter, that you are all out on such a terrible night?"

"Miss Estelle, the storm is raging!" another man cried. "And we haven't yet gathered in our crops. Our fields will be flooded. We'll all starve!"

There was a murmur of agreement from the rest of the crowd.

"Please help us, Miss Estelle!" begged John Miller.

Estelle looked up at the sky and then nodded once. "I will create a protection charm for the village which will save you and your crops from harm," she said firmly. "Go home, quickly now, and trust in me!"

"Bless you, Miss Estelle, and thank you!" John Miller said gratefully, as the crowd of villagers began to hurry away.

Paige, Shannon and Summer watched Estelle close the door as another girl, with the same dark hair, wearing a blue dress and gold jewellery, hurried through the entrance hall towards her.

"That's Eliza," Shannon said. "She's the one who's getting married."

"Estelle, what keeps you?" Eliza called impatiently. "The dancing is about to begin. Who was at the door?"

34

"Look!" Paige gasped, pointing at the gold necklace round Eliza Charm's neck. "That must be the Eye of Heaven!"

Set in the middle of the necklace was a large, sparkling blue stone.

"It was some of the villagers," Estelle told her sister. "I have promised them a charm to protect them from the storm. But such a powerful charm needs a powerful item to house its power. Give me the Eye of Heaven."

The girls watched as Eliza unclasped the necklace and handed it to Estelle. Estelle held it up as lightning crashed around the house, illuminating the hall with flashes of silver.

Estelle murmured an incantation under her breath, but Paige, Shannon and Summer couldn't hear what she said. As she finished, one of the lightning bolts seemed to hit the very centre of the necklace, making the sapphire dazzle with blue fire.

"It is done!" Estelle said, suddenly looking very tired and pale. "I have cast a powerful spell – a protection charm – into the sapphire. The jewel is now enchanted. But it must never leave the village

35

or the area will no longer be protected. I must find a hiding place that nobody will ever discover!"

"Your spell has left you exhausted," Eliza said anxiously. "Lean on me, sister. I will help you.' She put her arm around Estelle and led her from the hall, as the picture faded.

"And Estelle's protection charm worked," said the voice of the virtual narrator. "The storm skirted the village, and thus the crops were saved!"

The video clip began to fade. Paige, Summer and Shannon watched eagerly, but nothing else appeared and the screen went dark.

Summer opened her mouth to say something, but before she could do so, the door of the computer room swung open. Paige saw the tip of Velvet's tail disappear behind the printer as Miss Linnet looked into the room.

"Girls, it's very late!" the headmistress said crisply. "And you're here outside of the set times for using the computer room. I assume you have a teacher's permission?"

"Yes, Miss Linnet," Paige replied. "Mrs Stockbridge said we could use the computer this evening, although we didn't mean to stay so late."

"We lost track of the time. Sorry," Shannon added.

Miss Linnet raised her eyebrows. "You must be working on something very interesting!"

"It's about the history of Charm Hall," explained Summer.

Miss Linnet smiled. "That *does* sound fascinating, girls," she replied. "But you should go to bed now, or Mrs Bloomfield will not be pleased."

"Yes, Miss Linnet," the three girls muttered sheepishly.

The headmistress nodded and went on down the corridor. Quickly Paige turned to close the computer down. As she did so, she noticed that there was no web address in the address bar. "Summer's right," she said. "Velvet must have made that website appear by magic!"

At that moment, Velvet popped out from behind the printer. *Mew!* she added, jumped down and trotted out of the room.

"I think that means get a move on!" Paige grinned. "We'll see you upstairs, Velvet!"

The girls ran upstairs to their dorm as fast as they could.

"You're very quiet, Summer," Shannon panted as they passed the stone gargoyle at the bottom of the last flight of stairs. "What's up?"

"I think I've got a surprise for you guys," Summer said mysteriously.

"What is it?" asked Paige.

"I don't want to say until I've checked," Summer replied.

"Summer," Shannon groaned crossly. "Now you're making me really curious. That's not fair!"

Summer laughed. "It won't take a minute," she said.

The girls hurried into their dorm to find Velvet already curled up on Paige's bed.

"I wish we knew your secret for getting around so quickly, Velvet," Shannon grinned, grabbing her pyjamas. "Now tell us what's going on, Summer!"

Summer had gone over to her desk and was rummaging around in one of the drawers.

"Quick, Summer! Mrs Bloomfield will be doing her rounds in a minute to check everyone's in bed," Paige said, reaching for her pyjamas too.

Shannon was flapping around trying to get changed at top speed. She almost fell over as she accidentally put both feet down one leg of her pyjama bottoms. "What *are* you looking for, Summer?" she asked.

"This!" Summer declared triumphantly. And she held up an old brown leather journal.

"You mean that dusty old book we found in the cellars when we were looking for stuff to sell at the school fête last term?" Shannon shook her head. "Why are you so interested in *that*?"

"Yes, the writing was all smudged and faded, remember?" Paige added in a muffled voice as she pulled her pyjama top on over her head.

"Well, I think we should try reading it again," Summer replied in a determined voice, "because I think this is Estelle Charm's journal!"

"No way!" Shannon gasped. "You mean the one that was mentioned on the website?"

Summer nodded. She pointed at the book's cracked leather spine. *E* and *C* were imprinted there in very faded red letters.

"Estelle Charm!" Paige said, her voice shaking with excitement.

Summer laid the book on her desk and opened it. Shannon and Paige crowded round, trying to

39

decipher the writing on the first page, while Summer threw on her pyjamas.

"'This is a record of my family and all that I hold dear,'" Paige read aloud.

"Come on," Shannon said, turning out the light and grabbing her torch. "This could take a while and we'll be in big trouble if Mrs Bloomfield catches us. Everybody under Summer's duvet!"

The three girls dived underneath the duvet, taking the book with them. Shannon shone the torch on to a page of the journal. The writing was small and cramped and very faded in places.

Monday, this 7th day of June

The cook has been complaining that a full jug of cream in the larder is now half empty. I suspect my naughty brother James has been stealing cream again and giving it to Petal. It is no surprise that Petal's coat is so sleek and shiny. She must be the best-fed cat in the whole village!

"I can't see any mention of the Eye of Heaven," Shannon said in a disappointed voice a few minutes later, as they made their way painstakingly through another two or three of the diary entries. Some of the language was very old-fashioned, and the girls

had to skip quite a few words they simply didn't understand. In one entry, Estelle described a visit to see a neighbouring family. In another, a new dress was made for her by the village seamstress.

Summer turned another page.

Tuesday, this 15th day of June

Eliza is to be married to Captain Benedict! We will hold a ball to celebrate their engagement . . .

"Look at this." Shannon pointed further down the page. "'A recipe for wart removal'!"

"'Find a patch of strong green nettles in the

hedgerow. Pick the leaves and boil them with a pinch of nutmeg. Mix in . . .'" Paige frowned. "I can't make out the other ingredients."

"Look, the writing gets clearer again at the bottom of the page," Summer pointed out.

"'Rub this ointment on the offending wart and within three days it will drop off and be no more'!" Paige read on.

Suddenly, the sound of footsteps coming along the corridor made all three girls jump.

"It's Mrs Bloomfield!" Shannon whispered.

Paige, Shannon and Summer huddled together under the duvet, Shannon fumbling to switch off her torch. Paige felt her heart thumping like a drum as she waited for Mrs Bloomfield to pass.

But the footsteps stopped right outside their door. Paige held her breath. *Has Mrs Bloomfield heard something?* she wondered. *Is she going to come in?*

Chapter Five

After a moment, Mrs Bloomfield moved on. Paige heaved a huge sigh of relief.

"We'd better go straight to sleep now," Summer said firmly. "I've had enough excitement for one night, thank you!"

Paige nodded and she and Shannon hurried over to their own beds.

Shannon grinned. "Do you remember when Olivia Chandler's dorm was having a midnight feast?" she said. "They were sitting in the dark and they hadn't made a single sound, when Mrs Bloomfield suddenly burst in. She'd smelled their

43

cheese and onion crisps out on the landing!"

Paige and Summer started laughing, and Paige had to muffle her face in her pillow. She was beginning to feel drowsy. At the end of her bed Velvet was already sleeping soundly, a warm, soft weight on Paige's toes.

Paige closed her eyes.

"We'll look at the journal again tomorrow morning," she heard Summer whisper, just before she drifted off to sleep.

"You didn't see the look on Miss Arnold's face when she saw my clay pot. I've never seen someone try so hard not to laugh!" Shannon told Paige and Summer as they carried their lunch trays across the dining hall. It was the following day and the girls had just finished an art lesson. "She really had to bite her lip to stop herself!"

"Well, it *was* quite a strange shape," Summer pointed out tactfully.

"You mean because it didn't in any way look like a clay pot?" laughed Shannon. "I'm sure someone had turned up the speed on the potter's wheel before I used it!"

"Shall we go and sit on the terrace?" asked Paige. "The sun's out at the moment."

The girls went outside to find that most of the terrace benches were full of other pupils enjoying the autumn sunshine.

"Anyway, I was talking to Miss Arnold about the decorations for the Hallowe'en party," Shannon went on. "And she said we could make some clay pumpkins in our pottery class and then paint them orange. They'll be just like real pumpkins, with cut-out faces, and candles inside them."

"Oh, that's a good idea," Paige said. "Look, there's one table left over there."

They headed towards it.

"Pumpkins get thrown away after Hallowe'en, but we could keep the clay ones to use again year after year," Shannon went on. "Miss Arnold said that pumpkins are always a real winner when it comes to Hallowe'en."

At that moment, Abigail Carter pushed past the girls, carrying her own lunch tray, and zoomed straight over to the empty bench. She sat herself down, grinning triumphantly.

"Abigail, that's not fair!" Shannon said

indignantly. "You knew we were going to sit there."

Abigail smirked. "Well, some people are losers and some people are winners. I'm definitely a winner and so I get the bench! Sorry!"

"Look, those girls are leaving," Paige said as Shannon glared at Abigail.

The three friends hurried over to the free bench at the other end of the terrace.

"You know, we'd better start making our Hallowe'en costumes soon," said Paige, picking up her knife and fork. "We've been so busy with our history project, we haven't done much about them."

"And we must have another look at Estelle's journal," said Summer. "Maybe we'll have time during homework period."

"I wonder where Estelle hid the Eye of Heaven," said Paige thoughtfully. "Do you think the charm is still protecting the school and the village?"

Shannon was still staring at Abigail, who'd now been joined by her dorm-mate Mia. "Something's going on over there," Shannon said curiously. "Abigail's getting quite excited!"

Paige and Summer took a look. Abigail had become very animated and she was waving her

hands around as she talked. Mia was looking
a bit bewildered, but she was nodding her head
every so often.

After lunch, the girls went off to collect their
books for afternoon lessons. They were walking
past Miss Linnet's office when the headmistress
herself suddenly came out.

"Oh, hello, girls," she said. "I was just on my
way to the staff-room, but I do need to speak
with you rather urgently. Will you come into my
office, please?"

"You don't think that Miss Linnet has somehow
found out about Velvet staying in our dorm, do
you?" Shannon whispered to Paige and Summer.

Paige bit her lip. She hoped not. Miss Linnet
would not be pleased if she had found out. The girls
filed into the head's office.

"Girls, I know someone who could help with
your project," Miss Linnet went on, and Paige
breathed a sigh of relief. "She's called Mrs Brightman
and she lives right here in the village. She's retired
now, but she used to teach at Charm Hall."

"That sounds great, Miss Linnet," said Paige
eagerly.

"I've spoken to Mrs Brightman and she's happy to meet with you," Miss Linnet went on. "I've arranged for Sam, the caretaker, to escort you to her cottage after lessons today. He'll be waiting for you outside the front door in the minibus. You'll miss your homework period, but you can catch up later before dinner."

"Oh, that means I won't be able to email my parents," Paige said anxiously, realizing that they wouldn't be back before the computer room was out of bounds. "And it's Mum's birthday today."

"Then you have my permission to pop into the computer room for twenty minutes when you get back, Paige," said Miss Linnet. "Just keep your eye on the clock this time!"

"Thank you, Miss Linnet," Paige said gratefully as they left the office.

"We'll have to wait to look at the journal until after we've seen Mrs Brightman, then," said Summer.

"Talking of our project," Shannon said, glancing at the clock, "hadn't we better get a move on? We're late for history."

Clutching their books, the girls rushed off, arriving seconds before Mrs Stockbridge. Paige noticed that Abigail had gone back to her original seat on the other side of the room. Whatever she'd been up to, maybe it was over now.

"Girls, I'm going to give you some time today to work on your projects," Mrs Stockbridge announced. "Please split up into your groups. I'll come round and chat to you about how you're getting on."

"I should have brought the journal with me," remarked Summer with a frown.

"Never mind, we've got plenty to be getting on with," Shannon said, pulling out her notepad. "Why don't we make a list of everything we've found out so far?"

"Good idea," Paige agreed.

The girls were deep in a discussion about Estelle Charm when Mrs Stockbridge joined them.

"I can see you're very busy," the teacher said lightly, glancing at Shannon's list of notes. "How is it going?"

"We've found out *loads* of information about Estelle, who was one of Lavinia Charm's ancestors," Shannon replied. "And then there's the Eye of Heaven."

"The Eye of Heaven?" Mrs Stockbridge repeated with a smile. "Whatever's that?"

"It's a famous sapphire," Summer chipped in. "It belonged to the Charm family, but no one's seen it for *ages*. We think Estelle hid it!"

"Miss Linnet's arranged for us to go to the village and see Mrs Brightman, who used to teach here," Paige added. "We're hoping she might know stories about the sapphire."

"This sounds like great material for your project, girls!" Mrs Stockbridge said enthusiastically. "Where did you find all this information?"

"On the Internet," Shannon replied.

"Well, I hope you've been keeping a note of all the websites you've used," Mrs Stockbridge said, looking enquiringly at Shannon. "It's very important when you're doing a research project to keep all your references."

Shannon's face fell. Paige knew exactly what her friend was thinking. They couldn't tell Mrs Stockbridge about the most useful website, as it had been created by Velvet's magic.

"We, er, can't remember the web address, Mrs Stockbridge," Paige said quickly. A flash of irritation crossed the teacher's face. "But we'll write down *all* the ones we use in future," Paige added.

"And we've got some other really good research material as well," Summer piped up quickly.

Mrs Stockbridge raised her eyebrows, looking rather intrigued, and Paige guessed that Summer was going to explain about the journal. But at that moment, Olivia Chandler, who was sitting by the door, let out a squeal.

"Ooh, look! It's a *kitten!*"

Paige looked round and could hardly believe her eyes as she saw Velvet bound into the room. Purring loudly, the kitten trotted over to the teacher's desk and leaped up on to it.

"My goodness!" Mrs Stockbridge exclaimed. "Where did *you* come from, kitty?"

"I think she's from the farm down the lane," Shannon said quickly, glancing at Paige and Summer in alarm. "We've seen her around the school grounds occasionally."

"Oh, she's so cute!" said Penny Harris, and several of the girls started cooing and holding out their hands towards the kitten. Some of them got out of their seats to have a better look.

51

"I'm sure I've seen that cat before," Paige heard Abigail say in a low voice. And Paige realized that they had to get Velvet out of the classroom before Abigail started asking some awkward questions.

"Yes, she *is* very cute, but she doesn't belong in my history class!" Mrs Stockbridge said firmly, moving towards the kitten. As Mrs Stockbridge got closer, Velvet suddenly jumped down and darted swiftly out of the room.

Paige frowned. Velvet had never appeared in any of their classes before. So why had she suddenly trotted into their history class in full view of everyone? It had to mean something.

Paige turned to Shannon and Summer. "Don't mention Estelle's journal!" she whispered fiercely. "I think Velvet was trying to stop us from telling Mrs Stockbridge about it!"

Chapter Six

Shannon and Summer stared at Paige in amazement. But before the girls had time to discuss it further, Mrs Stockbridge turned back to them.

"Now, before that little interruption, you were going to tell me more about your research material," Mrs Stockbridge said, glancing enquiringly at Summer. "What were you going to say?"

Paige looked anxiously at Summer. What would her friend do?

"I'm sorry, Mrs Stockbridge," Summer replied, shaking her head. "It's gone straight out of my head!"

Mrs Stockbridge shrugged. "Oh, well, maybe it will come back to you," she said with a smile. "If it does, let me know."

"You were brilliant, Summer!" Paige said in a low voice as Mrs Stockbridge moved on to the next group. "You didn't give away a thing!"

"I think you're right, Paige," Summer whispered excitedly. "Velvet didn't want Mrs S to know about Estelle's journal! But why?"

"Maybe we'll have to read the rest of it to find out," suggested Shannon.

"We'll get right on it after we've been to see Mrs Brightman," Paige said.

When afternoon classes were over, the girls hurried to the school gates.

Sam was waiting for them. "Ah, here you are," he said gruffly. "We'd better hurry; Mrs Brightman's expecting you. She's a nice old lady and we don't want to keep her waiting."

"Do you know her?" asked Shannon, as they climbed into one of the school minibuses.

Sam nodded. "I've lived in the village all my life," he said as they drove down the long, tree-lined drive. "I remember Mrs Brightman teaching at the school. She and her husband live in the old village."

"So where does the old village end and the new village begin?" Paige asked curiously.

They had turned out of the drive now, passing a few cottages and the little shop where the girls bought Velvet's food.

"Well, I'll be able to show you in a minute," Sam said. And a moment later, as they reached the village green, Sam pointed out of the window. "This is the *old* village," he told Paige, indicating the pretty thatched cottages that were clustered around the green. "The *new* village stretches on from that huge old oak tree over there."

At the far end of the green Paige could see the majestic oak tree swaying slightly in the breeze, its leaves turning to autumn colours.

"That tree marks the boundary," said Sam.

Beyond it, Paige could see more modern houses and the shops of the new village.

Sam drove round to the other side of the green and down a pretty, winding lane lined with more cottages. "That's Mrs Brightman's house, the one with the blue curtains," Sam told the girls. He glanced at his watch. "I'll be back to fetch you in an hour."

The girls jumped out of the minibus and walked up the path to the front door.

Mrs Brightman opened the door, smiling warmly. She was white-haired and leaning on a stick. "So you're Paige, Summer and Shannon!" she exclaimed. "Which is which?"

The girls introduced themselves.

"Come in," Mrs Brightman urged. "I've made some tea and a big iced fruit cake, just waiting to be eaten up!"

"Oh, great!" Shannon said happily.

Soon the girls were settled in the tiny living room with cups of tea and generous slices of fruit cake.

"Miss Linnet tells me you're doing a history project about Charm Hall," Mrs Brightman said, her blue eyes bright in her wrinkled face. "And she thinks I might be able to help you."

"We hope so!" Paige said eagerly, reaching into her bag for her notepad. "Can you tell us anything about Lavinia Charm, or the rumours that her ancestors were witches?"

The elderly lady smiled. "Well, I knew Lavinia when I was a pupil at the school and then later, when I became a teacher. She was a *very* special person."

"How do you mean?" Shannon asked.

"Somehow Lavinia always seemed to know what was happening in the school *all* the time, even when she was away," Mrs Brightman explained. "It was always quite accepted that, whatever you did, whatever you tried to keep secret, Miss Charm would somehow find out all about it! Whether you were a pupil *or* a teacher!

"Of course, when I was a pupil at the school, my friends and I used to think Lavinia herself was a witch!" Mrs Brightman went on cheerfully. "We'd heard the rumours about the Charm women having magical powers. But, of course, as I got older, I realized that that was all nonsense!"

"So nothing magical ever happened while you were at the school?" asked Summer.

Mrs Brightman frowned. "Well, something rather strange did happen – but it was less to do with magic and more to do with luck!" she replied. "It was during the Second World War, when I was a pupil there. The manor was used as a refuge for evacuees from London." Her eyes took on a faraway look. "Anyway, one night an enemy plane flew over. We think he may have got lost because we'd never been the target of a bombing raid before. But that plane dropped bombs on the school and the village. I can still remember the terrible noise . . ." Her voice died away.

"What happened?" Paige asked.

"Miraculously, every single bomb missed its target!" Mrs Brightman said, shaking her head in wonder. "No one in the school or the village was harmed. It was sheer good luck!"

Or it was Estelle's charm that protected them! Paige thought.

"I have some photos from my time at the school which you might like to see," Mrs Brightman went on, showing them a large album bound in faded red velvet. She opened it, and the girls gathered round eagerly.

"These are my class photos," Mrs Brightman said, turning the pages slowly.

In one of the photos Paige noticed a black cat peeping round the legs of one of the girls. On the next page she spotted the cat in another picture, sitting on a tree stump and watching a group of girls playing tennis. The cat looked just like Velvet; even down to the plum velvet collar around its neck.

"Is that the cat in Lavinia Charm's portrait?" Paige asked, pointing it out to Shannon and Summer.

Mrs Brightman nodded. "It's Lavinia's cat, Jewel," she explained. "She was a lovely cat, and a very important member of the school. I remember she loved wandering about on her own, and she used to pop up in the strangest of places!"

Paige grinned at Shannon and Summer. She could guess what they were thinking: *Just like Velvet!*

"Mrs Brightman, do you know anything about Estelle Charm or the Eye of Heaven?" asked Summer.

"I don't know much about Estelle," Mrs Brightman replied, "except that Lavinia was descended from Estelle's younger brother, James. But I've heard of the Eye of Heaven." She frowned. "No one knows where it is, but I think a lot of people would love to find it! While I was a teacher at the school, there were several attempted burglaries. The manor was ransacked, but nothing was actually taken. Lavinia was certain the thieves were looking for the Eye of Heaven."

Just then the doorbell rang.

"That will be Sam," Mrs Brightman said, closing the photo album. "It's been such a treat to talk to you about the old days, girls! I haven't met anyone as interested in the history of Charm Hall since little Susan Chadwell, a pupil of mine some years ago. She was very intrigued by the Eye of Heaven."

"Thanks for your time, Mrs Brightman. We'll let you know if we find out any more," Summer promised.

Sam was waiting for the girls outside. He drove them back to the school and dropped them at the front entrance.

"I've just got time to email my mum before dinner," Paige said to Shannon and Summer. "I'll see you in the dining hall."

"OK," said Shannon.

Summer grinned. "We won't look at Estelle's journal without you!" she said.

Paige hurried off to the computer room, all the things Mrs Brightman had told them whirling around inside her head. Obviously some people believed that the Eye of Heaven was hidden in Charm Hall itself, and that was why there had been burglaries over the years. *But*, Paige thought, *Estelle could have hidden it anywhere . . .*

The door of the computer room was closed. Paige's heart sank as she guessed that the room had been locked up for the evening. She turned the handle anyway, and, to her relief, the door opened.

Mrs Stockbridge was sitting at one of the desks, staring intently at a monitor. To Paige's surprise, the teacher was browsing one of the websites about Charm Hall that Paige and her friends had been looking at the day before.

Suddenly Mrs Stockbridge realized that someone else was in the room. She swung round, looking rather guilty. "Oh, Paige, it's you!"

"Sorry if I disturbed you, Mrs Stockbridge," Paige said.

"That's OK," Mrs Stockbridge replied, swiftly closing the computer down. "But, Paige, I'm afraid the computer session's over for today."

"Miss Linnet said it was OK for me to email my mum. It's her birthday," Paige explained.

"Fine," Mrs Stockbridge said with a smile. "I'll leave you to it then. Don't be late for dinner."

And she swept out of the room.

Frowning, Paige stared after her. Why had Mrs Stockbridge been looking at websites on Charm Hall? And, more strangely, why had she looked so guilty about it?

Chapter Seven

"Maybe Mrs Stockbridge was trying to track down our references for us," Summer said thoughtfully.

Paige had quickly emailed her parents and then joined Shannon and Summer in the dining hall. While they were eating dinner, she'd told them all about the teacher's strange behaviour.

"That's true," Paige agreed. "She did say it was important to keep track of all our research."

"Yes, but why would she look guilty?" Shannon asked. "She's taking our project a bit seriously, isn't she?"

"We'd better make sure we keep a note of all our sources in future," said Paige.

"And now we'd better go and get on with our costumes," Shannon added, pushing her empty plate away. "Otherwise, we'll have nothing to wear to the Hallowe'en party."

"I think it's about time we read a bit more of Estelle's journal," Summer said, as the three friends finished dinner on Friday evening a week later. "We've done so much work on our costumes lately that we've hardly looked at the journal."

"Why don't we take it to the library now?" suggested Paige. "We can use the dictionary to help us with the old-fashioned words."

"Good idea!" Summer and Shannon agreed.

Summer went to fetch the journal, while Paige and Shannon went straight to the library. The room was large and spacious with book-lined walls and rows of desks and chairs, as well as big leather armchairs which were perfect for curling up in with a good book.

"Good, there's no one else here," Shannon remarked as she went to fetch the dictionary. Then suddenly she burst out laughing. "I was wrong! There *is* someone here!"

Paige was puzzled, she couldn't see anyone. Curiously she followed Shannon over to the bookshelves. Then she spotted Velvet curled up neatly on one of the leather chairs, her paws tucked underneath her.

"Hi, Velvet!" Paige smiled, tickling the kitten under her chin.

"Here's the dictionary," said Shannon, pulling a large, leather-bound book off the shelves.

They sat down at a desk to wait for Summer. Velvet uncurled herself and strolled over, jumping up on to the desk beside them. A few moments later Summer hurried in, the journal tucked under her arm, and closed the door behind her.

"I think we'd got to this page," Summer said, joining Paige and Shannon at the table and opening the journal.

"'Today James had a lucky escape,'" Summer read slowly. "'He fell into the village pond and almost drowned! The silly boy was catching tadpoles and he tumbled in. He cannot swim and there was no one around to hear his cries for help.

Luckily Tom Merry, the blacksmith, passed by a moment later and pulled James to safety. He brought James home and we put him straight to bed. He is shivering, and I pray he does not come down with an ague.' "

"What's that?" asked Paige.

Shannon looked up the word. "It means a fever," she announced.

" 'I have given him a medicinal potion of agrimony and bergamot to drink,' " Summer read on. " 'And I hope that this will protect him from sickness. We could not bear to lose our dear, naughty James!' "

"Agrimony and bergamot are kinds of herbs," said Shannon, poring over the dictionary pages.

"Look, there are some more recipes here.' Summer said, turning the page.

" 'How to mend a broken leg,' " Paige read out. " 'A potion of herbs for curing spots and boils'. 'A charm to ward off fleas'!"

The girls laughed.

"Here's another journal entry," said Summer, pointing at the opposite page. "Oh, it's about Eliza's engagement party!"

"Read it, Summer," Shannon urged, resting her elbows on the dictionary.

"'Tonight we shall make merry for Eliza is engaged to Captain Benedict! The house has been decorated with flowers and the cook has been busy all day. We are to have roast chicken and syllabub. Eliza is very excited because tonight at the ball she will be wearing the Eye of Heaven for the very first time.'" Summer frowned. "Look, there's a break here," she pointed out. "And then Estelle starts writing again, lower down the page."

"Her handwriting's changed," said Paige, puzzled. "This top part is quite neat, but the bottom entry is really untidy."

Summer began to read the entry aloud, but very slowly as she tried to make out the words. "'The party was wonderful. But just as the dancing was about to begin, there was a knock at the door. The villagers were worried about a terrible storm that was threatening to destroy their crops. So I cast a protection charm, a charm that now lies deep within the Eye of Heaven, and I have hidden it carefully inside the house. And now I must rest because casting the charm has left me weary . . .'"

Summer broke off. "The next sentence is so faded, I can't read it!" she exclaimed.

"Let me see," said Shannon, and she and Paige bent over the journal. But Summer was right. The words were illegible.

Velvet had jumped to her feet. She pushed her face against Paige's shoulder as Paige bent over the book.

"It's impossible to work out!" Shannon sighed, still squinting at the words.

A golden shimmer suddenly caught Paige's eye. She turned her head slightly and, with a thrill of excitement, saw that Velvet's whiskers were glowing with the familiar golden shimmer.

The golden gleam seemed to spill from Velvet's whiskers on to the page of Estelle's journal. The words that the girls had not been able to make out now began to glow too.

"That's Velvet's magic!" Summer breathed.

The girls watched with mounting excitement as the words became clearer and clearer until they were a pure, glowing gold.

" 'The Eye of Heaven lies with the beast who cannot see,' " Shannon read aloud.

"So we know that Estelle probably hid the Eye of

Heaven somewhere in Charm Hall, and this is her clue to exactly where," Summer said.

"But what does Estelle mean?" Paige murmured. "What is the 'beast who cannot see'?"

Shannon and Summer looked equally puzzled.

"Maybe it's some sort of code," Shannon suggested.

Summer opened her mouth to say something, but at that moment Velvet leaped off the desk and bounded over to the library door, which was standing slightly ajar.

Paige frowned. She remembered Summer closing the door when she came in with the journal, so why was it open again? Curiously, Paige jumped up and followed Velvet to the door. As she got there, she heard the sound of footsteps running off down the corridor.

Chapter Eight

Paige pulled the door open wide and peered out into the passage. She couldn't see anyone now, but there had definitely been somebody there.

"What's the matter, Paige?" asked Shannon. She and Summer were still bent over Estelle's journal.

"I think someone's been listening to our conversation," Paige said, frowning. "The door was open."

Summer looked worried. "I definitely closed it when I came in," she said.

"Did you see anyone, Paige?" Shannon asked.

Paige shook her head. "It was too dark, and they

71

ran off when they heard me coming."

"Maybe it was our shadow," suggested Shannon.

"Abigail?" Paige frowned. "But she's stopped following us now, hasn't she?"

Shannon didn't look convinced. "Who else could it be?" she asked. "Do you think she heard anything about the sapphire?"

"I hope not!" said Paige.

"Even if she did, I don't think she would have known what we were talking about," Summer said reassuringly.

Paige thought back over their conversation, as Velvet wound herself lovingly around Paige's legs. Summer was right; even if Abigail had overheard something, she wouldn't have a clue who Estelle was or what the Eye of Heaven could be.

"I think we should all make a pact not to talk about the journal in public from now on," Summer said seriously. "I mean, if the Eye of Heaven *is* hidden somewhere in Charm Hall, we don't want everyone to know about it, do we?"

Paige shook her head and bent down to stroke Velvet. "Remember what Mrs Brightman said?" she pointed out. "That there were break-ins because thieves were looking for the sapphire? We don't want that to happen again!"

"Yes, we have to make sure the Eye of Heaven stays right here!" Shannon said in a very determined voice. "That's what Estelle would have wanted."

"Why, oh, why did I decide to go as a werewolf?" Paige wailed, as she and Shannon rushed to their Hallowe'en party committee meeting the following day. "I'm sick of all that fake fur!"

The girls had spent the morning working on their party costumes. It was Saturday and there was only a week to go before Hallowe'en.

"Well, what about me?" Shannon laughed. "I still have to find a way to put a fake bolt through my neck, so that I can go as Frankenstein's monster!"

"Summer had the right idea with her Dracula outfit," Paige said, laughing. "All she needs to do is buy a set of fangs and some fake blood! She said that she might even be able to finish off her cloak today, once she's back from gym practice."

"Well, however long our costumes take, it'll all be worthwhile," Shannon said firmly. "Especially since we're going to be allowed to go trick or treating on Hallowe'en."

Paige grinned. Miss Linnet had announced that, as well as a prize for the best costume, the girls would be able to dress up and go trick or treating down in the new village before the party.

Shannon suddenly slowed down and dropped her voice. "I know we *think* Abigail's stopped following us around . . ." she said, glancing over her shoulder, ". . . but do you ever get the feeling that we're still being watched?"

"Yes," Paige agreed. "But maybe we're just jumpy because of what happened in the library last night."

Shannon nodded, but before she could say anything, Mrs Stockbridge, who was one of the teachers on the party committee, came round the corner. She was carrying three large rolls of black crêpe paper.

"Hello, girls," she said. "Look what my husband gave me from the paper mill where he works."

"That will be great for witches' hats!" Shannon said enthusiastically.

Mrs Stockbridge nodded. "I just hope there's enough to go round!" she laughed as they went into the classroom where the meeting was being held. "From what I hear, half the girls in the school are dressing up as witches! And, talking of witches, how is your project about the Charm witches coming along?"

The girls didn't have time to reply because Miss Linnet came into the classroom then, and the meeting got underway. The plans for the party menu were finalized, and then they discussed what materials were still needed for the decorations.

"Everything's going well, thanks to all your hard work!" Miss Linnet declared at the end of the meeting. "Now, Mrs Stockbridge and Miss Collins have kindly volunteered to drive the committee members down to the new village to buy the last few things that we need. So please be in the lobby in ten minutes."

A quarter of an hour later, Paige, Shannon and the rest of the committee were on the minibus, heading for the shops.

"Shock, horror!" Shannon whispered to Paige, clutching her heart and pretending to faint. "Where's Abigail? Don't tell me she decided not to come!"

Paige glanced round. Mia was sitting behind them, but Abigail was nowhere to be seen. "That's weird, isn't it?" Paige said with a frown. "I would have thought she'd have made sure she was right at the front with Mrs Stockbridge!"

"Yes, bossing everyone else around and taking over!" Shannon agreed. She looked round. "Hey, Mia! Where's Abigail?"

"Oh, she's busy," Mia replied, looking slightly uncomfortable. "She stayed behind in our dorm."

"Hmm, I wonder what Abigail's up to," Shannon whispered to Paige.

As the minibus drove through the old village, Paige glanced over at the oak tree, remembering what Sam had told them about how it marked the boundary between the old and new villages. The new village wouldn't have existed during Estelle Charm's time, Paige realized, so it probably wasn't protected from harm by the Eye of Heaven as the school and the old village were.

Mrs Stockbridge parked in the new village high street, which was lined with shops. They stopped at the greengrocer's to place an order for some pumpkins, and then they went into the craft shop next door. By the time they came out, laden with bags, it was raining hard.

"Oh, dear," said Mrs Stockbridge with a frown. "We've still got a few more things to get. Miss Collins, why don't you take the girls into the hardware store? I'll pop home and get a few umbrellas. I only live in the next street." She glanced at Shannon and Paige. "You two can come and help me."

Paige and Shannon followed Mrs Stockbridge down a side road which led away from the high street to a small estate of modern houses. They were sheltering under the tiny porch while the teacher fumbled for her key, when, suddenly, the door opened.

"Oh, thank you, Graham!" said Mrs Stockbridge gratefully. "Girls, this is my husband."

Paige and Shannon smiled politely at the tall, fair-haired man as he ushered them into the hall.

"This is Paige and Shannon. They're in my history class," Mrs Stockbridge went on. She had opened a cupboard under the stairs and was rummaging around inside. "We're shopping in the village for the Hallowe'en party."

"Nice to meet you," Mr Stockbridge said, smiling.

"Actually, Graham's very interested in old buildings," Mrs Stockbridge explained, emerging from the cupboard with three umbrellas. "He'd probably love to know what you've found out about Charm Hall. How is your project going, by the way, girls? You do know that they have to be handed in on Monday, don't you?"

"We've nearly finished, Mrs Stockbridge," Shannon replied.

"And I shall expect to see *all* your reference materials too," the teacher added.

Paige and Shannon glanced at each other.

"Oh, you will, Mrs Stockbridge," Paige assured her. *Apart from Estelle Charm's journal, of course*, she added silently.

"Class! Will you *please* be quiet!" Mrs Stockbridge said sharply. It was Monday and the girls were in their history lesson.

"Surely there's no need for all this noise?" Mrs Stockbridge went on. "You're only finishing off your projects. You shouldn't have much left to discuss."

The noise level died down for a few minutes, and Paige bent over their project notes. She was putting the pages they'd written in order. Meanwhile, Shannon was labelling the photos they'd taken of Charm Hall with Paige's digital camera, and Summer was putting the finishing touches to the title page.

"Which is the best one?" Shannon asked, holding up two photos of the outside of the school as the classroom gradually began to get noisier again. "I thought Summer could stick one on the title page."

"That one," Paige said, pointing to the one on the left.

"Yep, definitely," Summer agreed, taking the chosen picture. "I'll put it here, under the project title."

Suddenly Mrs Stockbridge was standing in front of their table, glaring at them. "Girls! Didn't you hear what I just said?" she snapped. "I asked for quiet, and you're still talking. You can all report for detention this afternoon after lessons!" And she turned and walked away.

Paige stared speechlessly at the teacher's back. She couldn't believe that Mrs Stockbridge had been so unfair! After all, they weren't the only girls in the class who'd been talking and they had been discussing their work. She glanced at Shannon and Summer, who looked just as surprised.

As the bell rang, each group went up to Mrs Stockbridge to hand in their project. Paige, Summer and Shannon were last.

"Go straight to classroom 11B after classes this afternoon," Mrs Stockbridge said, without even looking up from the essays she was marking. "Detention lasts for an hour."

"Well!" Shannon burst out when they'd left the classroom. "What's eating *her*? She's never been so mean before!"

"I know," Paige agreed as they went over to the stairs. "I can't believe she gave us detention!"

Summer frowned. "I don't think Mrs Stockbridge is as nice as we first thought," she remarked.

Abigail and Mia were standing chatting in the corridor as the girls passed by.

"Enjoy your detention, won't you?" Abigail called gloatingly.

Paige ignored her. Even Shannon didn't say anything. *That's got to be a first!* Paige thought.

When afternoon lessons were over, the

girls went up to their dorm to leave their books, and then walked reluctantly to classroom 11B. To Paige's dismay, Mrs Stark was seated at the teacher's desk.

"Mrs Stockbridge is busy," Mrs Stark said coolly, "so I'm taking detention for her. I suggest you do something more useful than writing lines. One of you can go and fetch your maths books."

"I'll go," Paige offered. Quickly she rushed upstairs, not wanting to annoy Mrs Stark by taking too long. She dashed into their dorm and stopped abruptly. It looked *different*.

Things have been moved! Paige thought, noticing that the penholder on her desk was now on the left side instead of the right. *Someone's been in our room!*

Suddenly Paige remembered the unknown person who had been eavesdropping outside the library door. Anxiously, she ran over to Summer's bedside table and looked in the drawer for Estelle Charm's journal.

It was gone.

Chapter Nine

"Oh, no!" Paige gasped.

She stood there gazing into the empty drawer in horror, until she remembered that Mrs Stark would be waiting for her. Quickly she grabbed the maths books and rushed out of the dorm.

As she clattered down the stairs, one question echoed in Paige's mind: was it Abigail who had stolen the journal?

Paige reached the bottom of the stairs and turned towards classroom 11B. But, as she hurried past the neighbouring classroom, she saw girls bent over chessboards through the open door. Suddenly

Paige came to a dead halt, because there was Abigail sitting at one of the tables with a girl called Lauren Brown.

"Abigail's at chess club!" Paige muttered to herself. She knew the club started straight after lessons were over. There was no way Abigail would have had time to go up to the girls' dorm and steal the journal *after* they'd been up there to leave their books. Paige frowned. Abigail *couldn't* be the thief – so who was it?

"Ah, Paige, we were just about to send out a search party for you," Mrs Stark said tartly as she arrived back at the classroom. "Do the sums on page thirty-seven, girls."

Paige bit her lip as she handed Summer and Shannon their maths books. She couldn't even tell them what had happened until detention was over.

The next forty-five minutes felt like the longest of Paige's life. She glanced at the clock so often that Mrs Stark eventually told her off. When the teacher finally said they were allowed to go, Paige immediately jumped to her feet. Ignoring Mrs Stark's disapproving stare, she rushed out into the corridor and waited impatiently for Shannon and Summer to join her.

"The journal's gone!" she exclaimed, the minute her friends arrived.

Summer turned pale. "I *wondered* what was up," she said. "You were itching to get out of there, Paige."

"Abigail!" Shannon said looking furious. "I knew she was up to no good, sneaking around after us!"

"Abigail's at chess club," Paige said quickly. "It couldn't have been her."

At that moment Mrs Stockbridge came along the corridor. She didn't even look at the girls as she went into classroom 11B.

"Thank you for covering the detention," the girls heard her say to Mrs Stark. "I would have done it myself, but I just had so much to sort out."

"Don't worry about it, Susan," replied Mrs Stark. "I was happy to help."

"What are we going to do now?" asked Shannon. "We have to get Estelle's journal back, but we have no idea who took it!"

Summer was staring into space, looking thoughtful. "You two go back to our dorm and have

84

a look for the journal, just in case I didn't put it away and left it on my bed, or something . . ." she said slowly.

"Where are *you* going?" asked Paige.

"I'll come and help you in a minute, but first I've got to check something in the library," Summer said mysteriously, and she hurried off.

Paige and Shannon glanced at each other and shrugged. Then they went upstairs and began to search their dorm, but there was no sign of the journal anywhere. They'd just finished looking under Summer's bed, when Summer herself burst in, waving a book.

"I know who took the journal!" she exclaimed.

"Abigail?" asked Shannon.

"No – Susan Chadwell!" Summer declared triumphantly.

Paige and Shannon both looked blankly at Summer for a moment.

"Oh, you mean that pupil Mrs Brightman mentioned. The girl who was so interested in the Eye of Heaven," Shannon said at last, looking bewildered. "But what's she got to do with this?"

Summer opened the book she was holding. As

she did so, Paige saw that it was a Charm Hall
School Yearbook from the 1970s.

Summer flipped through and stopped at one of
the class photos. "Look!" she said, pointing to a
student in the front row.

Puzzled, Paige stared at the dark-haired, green-
eyed girl. She looked vaguely familiar, but at first
Paige couldn't figure out why. Then, suddenly, she
recognized her. "I don't believe it!" Paige exclaimed.
"That's Mrs Stockbridge!"

"What?" Shannon peered at the photo more closely. "It *is* Mrs Stockbridge!" she agreed in amazement.

Summer nodded. "Mrs Stockbridge is Susan Chadwell," she confirmed.

Paige could feel the pieces of the jigsaw fitting into place. "Everything's starting to make sense now!" she declared.

"Yes," Shannon agreed. "Susan Chadwell, now known as Susan Stockbridge, is *still* looking for the Eye of Heaven after all these years!"

"That's why she was so interested in our project," Paige said. "And why I saw her researching Charm Hall on the computer!"

"It even explains why we got detention," Summer pointed out. "She needed time to come to our dorm and steal the journal!"

"And I bet she was the person listening outside the library door," Shannon added. "So what do we do now?"

The three girls looked at each other.

"We have to find the sapphire ourselves and keep it safe from Mrs Stockbridge," Paige said in a determined voice. "If she gets hold of it, the school and the old village won't be protected any longer."

"At least we can remember the clue," said Summer. " 'The Eye of Heaven lies with the beast who cannot see.' "

"Yes, but we still don't know what it means," Shannon said with a sigh. "What *is* this beast?"

"We need to solve the puzzle as fast as we can," Paige pointed out urgently. "Now that Mrs Stockbridge has the journal, she could read the clue herself, work out where the sapphire is hidden, and steal it!"

"I still can't believe Mrs Stockbridge could be so two-faced!" Shannon said crossly, as she, Paige and Summer climbed the stairs. They'd just been to dinner and the sight of Mrs Stockbridge at the teachers' table had put them off their food. "We thought she was so nice," Summer grumbled. "And all the time, she was just hoping our project research would lead her to the Eye of Heaven!"

"I hope she doesn't solve the riddle before we do," Paige said anxiously. Then suddenly she stopped and frowned. "Listen, I can hear purring!"

The girls glanced up, and there was Velvet. She

was perched on top of one of the stone gargoyles which lined the wall alongside this particular staircase. The gargoyle had bulging eyes, sharp fangs and large, protruding ears.

"Velvet, what are you doing up there?" Shannon laughed. "Come down!"

Velvet simply purred louder and began rubbing her furry cheeks against the gargoyle's ears.

Paige stared at the stone carving.

The Eye of Heaven lies with the beast who cannot see . . . she thought.

"Oh!" Paige turned to Summer and Shannon, her face alight with excitement. "The riddle – could 'the beast' be one of the school gargoyles?"

"They're certainly beastly!" Shannon agreed, looking at the gargoyle.

"But they have eyes," Summer pointed out.

"Maybe there's a blind one somewhere," Paige suggested eagerly. "There are lots of different ones all over the school."

"Inside *and* outside!" Shannon groaned. "We'd better start looking now!"

"Let's do the outside before we have to be indoors at eight," Summer suggested. "We'll need your torch, Shannon."

Velvet let out a cheerful *mew* and leaped down from her perch. She rushed up to the dorm room ahead of the girls and while Shannon found her torch Velvet settled herself comfortably on Paige's bed.

The girls hurried out into the darkness to check all the gargoyles. They began with the ones around the school entrance, and then they made their way round the whole of the school building, carefully checking the ones which were placed at intervals along the walls.

"Nothing here," Shannon said, shaking her head. "All these gargoyles can see."

"Let's look in the gardens," suggested Summer. "There's a fountain with a big gargoyle in the middle and smaller ones around the outside."

By eight o'clock the girls had been all around the gardens and they were chilled to the bone by an icy wind which had sprung up, but they hadn't found a single blind gargoyle.

"Well, at least we know it must be inside," Paige said. "Shall we keep looking?"

Shannon frowned. "We'd better be careful," she

pointed out. "There are a lot of people around, and we don't want Mrs Stockbridge to find out what we're up to."

"Let's sneak out and look tonight, when everyone else is in bed!" Paige suggested.

Shannon grinned and Summer nodded. "It's a plan!" said Shannon.

"Ready?" Paige whispered as she stood by the dorm door in the darkness.

"Ready!" Summer whispered, and Shannon waved her torch in the air. Velvet gave a mew and followed them as the girls slipped out of the door. They had timed this carefully, waiting until Mrs Bloomfield had made the last of her nightly rounds.

Velvet bounded silently towards the stairs and Paige, Shannon and Summer tiptoed after her. They'd already checked the gargoyles on the walls leading up to their dorm. But as they reached the bottom of the first flight of stairs, Velvet suddenly stopped. Her tail quivered and her ears pricked up. Quickly she darted into a nearby bathroom.

"Someone's coming!" Shannon whispered as they heard footsteps.

Hurriedly the girls followed Velvet into the bathroom and crouched out of sight in the shadows.

Mrs Bloomfield walked past, carrying a hot drink.

"She's supposed to have finished her rounds now and gone to bed," Shannon groaned quietly.

"Maybe she was just getting herself a bedtime drink," Summer suggested. "I just hope she doesn't open our door!"

Paige and Shannon nodded in agreement.

After a few moments, Velvet left the bathroom and Paige guessed that that meant it was safe for them to leave too. The girls crept along the corridors, checking for blind gargoyles by the light of Shannon's torch. They also looked in all the classrooms, but they dared not put the lights on in case they were spotted.

"Maybe the beast isn't a gargoyle at all," Paige sighed as they headed towards the library, Velvet still trotting along beside them.

"We can't give up yet!" said Shannon. "I think there are a couple of gargoyles in the library. Let's check them out."

Summer opened the library door and Shannon shone the torch around the room. There were a couple of gargoyles either side of the old fireplace, but both had big, clear eyes.

"Nothing," Shannon said disappointedly. "Let's carry on."

Paige turned to follow Shannon out of the library when Summer suddenly gave an exclamation.

"Look at Velvet's whiskers!"

Paige and Shannon spun round to see Velvet standing in front of them, her whiskers gleaming with a magical golden glow and her tail twitching from side to side.

"Velvet's telling us we're in the right place!" Summer whispered urgently.

"But we checked the gargoyles in here," Shannon pointed out, playing her torch over the walls again.

The golden light from Velvet's whiskers seemed to flow out away from the kitten in a cloud of sparks. Paige watched as the light moved up one wall to surround a hunched stone figure. "There!" she said, grabbing Shannon's arm. "Look, above the bookcase!"

Shannon focused the beam of torchlight on the

bookcase, and there at the top, the girls saw a stone gargoyle with his eyes screwed tightly shut.

"It's the beast who cannot see!" Shannon cried.

Quickly she handed the torch to Summer and rushed over to push the library stepladder across to the bookcase. As Paige and Summer watched, Shannon climbed up the steps. But the ladder was too short to reach the gargoyle, so, with a determined look on her face, Shannon put the torch down and began to clamber up the bookshelves.

"Shannon, be careful!" Summer said anxiously.

Shannon had reached the top now. Holding on to the bookcase with one hand, she began poking and prodding at the gargoyle with the other.

"There must be a secret compartment, or something," she panted. "This must be the right gargoyle. He definitely can't see!"

Shannon's elbow banged against the gargoyle's big nose, and it twisted slightly. There was a loud, creaking noise, and Paige and Summer gasped as the bookcase began to shake.

"Is this supposed to happen?" Shannon exclaimed, clinging to the bookshelves with both hands.

The bookcase was sliding aside like a door,
taking Shannon with it, and Paige could see some
kind of gap behind it. When the bookcase came to
a halt, Shannon scrambled back down to the floor
while Paige and Summer peered curiously into the
hole that the sliding bookcase had revealed.

Summer shone the torch beam into the hole, and
Paige saw that it stretched away into more darkness.

"It's a secret passage!" Summer whispered.

Chapter Ten

"Brilliant!" Shannon said triumphantly, joining her friends at the entrance to the passage.

Velvet slipped through the gap, followed by Paige, Summer and Shannon. They found themselves following a long, narrow corridor which twisted this way and that.

"This is like something out of a movie!" Paige whispered as they hurried along.

"Look, there's a door," Summer added, pointing ahead of them. There, at the end of the corridor, was a large wooden door with iron hinges. "I wonder what's behind it."

Paige cautiously reached out for the door handle and turned it. With a *creak*, the heavy door swung open. Shannon pointed her torch through the open doorway and Paige and Summer peered inside. Paige could hardly bear the excitement. What would they find? Was the Eye of Heaven behind the door, waiting for them?

"It's an empty room!" Shannon said disappointedly.

The girls and Velvet went through the doorway and looked around. Shannon was right. The room had panelled walls and flagstones on the floor, but there was nothing in it at all. Velvet crossed to the far side of the little room and then miaowed loudly at Paige.

Curiously, Paige went over to stroke the kitten, but as she crossed the floor she felt one of the flagstones shift under her weight. "Oh!" Paige murmured. "What's this?"

Quickly she called Summer and Shannon over and together the girls examined the stone. Velvet joined them, pawing at the edges of the stone insistently.

"It looks heavy," Shannon said. "But it's definitely loose."

"Let's try to lift it," Summer suggested.

The three girls wriggled their fingers down the sides of the stone and braced themselves to lift it. Shannon counted to three and then they all heaved together. Slowly, the flagstone lifted. The girls shifted it sideways and lowered it on to the floor.

"Look!" Paige whispered, hardly daring to believe her eyes. Underneath the flagstone lay a small, square wooden box.

"I think we've found the Eye of Heaven!" Summer breathed.

"Yes," Shannon agreed eagerly.

Paige picked up the box, which was beautifully carved with flowers and leaves, and carefully lifted the lid. "No!" she exclaimed, gazing despondently at the sumptuous red velvet lining. "It's empty!"

"It must have been Mrs Stockbridge!" Summer exclaimed, as they crept quickly back to their dorm. "She got there before us and took the sapphire."

"What are we going to do?" Shannon asked in a furious whisper. "Somehow we *have* to get the Eye of Heaven back!"

"How?" Summer asked, looking upset. "Even if

we told one of the other teachers, no one would believe *us* over Mrs Stockbridge!"

"There's got to be a way," Paige said determinedly as they reached their dorm. "We just haven't thought of it yet . . ."

The girls went straight to bed, although it took Paige a long time to get to sleep. A storm was raging outside and every time she felt herself drifting off to sleep, a crash of thunder would jolt her awake again. She lay awake for hours, thinking about the missing sapphire, and when she woke in the morning she felt heavy-eyed and tired.

"'Morning," Paige yawned, sitting up in bed and pushing her hair out of her eyes.

"You look like I feel, Paige!" Shannon groaned. "I was awake for hours wondering how we could get the sapphire back."

"Me too," put in Summer.

"And did either of you think of anything?" Paige asked hopefully.

Shannon and Summer both shook their heads glumly.

"We might as well get up now," said Summer,

climbing out of bed. "Then we can finish off our party costumes before breakfast."

"OK," Paige agreed. She was really looking forward to the Hallowe'en party on Saturday, but she knew she'd enjoy it a whole lot more if only they could get the Eye of Heaven back first.

When they reached the showers, the girls found that there was no hot water.

"Something must be wrong with the heating," Shannon commented. "The whole school is freezing!"

The girls took very quick cold showers and then went back to their dorm and finished off the last bits of their Hallowe'en costumes. Although they couldn't think about anything except how to get the Eye of Heaven out of Mrs Stockbridge's clutches, they didn't come up with a single plan. By the time they went down for breakfast, Paige was feeling quite disheartened.

"Sorry, girls," said Joan as they queued up in the dining hall. "It's cereal only today, I'm afraid. Lightning struck a tree in the night and it brought down the power lines, so now we've got no electricity."

"No scrambled eggs!" Shannon said dismally.

"No wonder the showers were cold," Paige put in.

Looking quite distracted, Joan handed out bowls of cornflakes.

"Are you OK, Joan?" Summer asked.

Joan sighed. "I was on my way to work this morning, and the engine of my car caught fire!" she sighed. "I had to leave it at the bottom of the drive. I don't even know if it can be fixed!"

Just then Olivia Chandler came up behind the girls. "Is it OK if I take a bowl of cereal for Rose?" she asked Joan. "She tripped and hurt her ankle this morning, and Mrs Bloomfield said she had to stay in the dorm."

"The school seems full of bad luck today!" Joan said, handing Olivia a bowl of cornflakes for her friend.

As Paige, Summer and Shannon sat down at a table to eat, Shannon's eyes suddenly widened. "Hey!" she exclaimed. "I've just realized why so many things are going wrong around here! It's because the Eye of Heaven is missing!"

"Yes, of course, Estelle's protection charm has

101

gone," Paige said, realizing her friend was right. "You know what? I bet Mrs Stockbridge has taken it home! She lives in the new village, which means that the school isn't protected any more."

"And neither is the old village," Summer pointed out. "That's where Joan lives. I expect that's why her car blew up!"

The three girls stared at each other in dismay.

"Which means that there's only one thing we can do," Shannon said, looking determined. "We have to ask Mrs Stockbridge to give the sapphire back!"

The girls didn't have a chance to confront Mrs Stockbridge until lessons were over for the day. Miss Linnet had called a special evening assembly to give them all the arrangements for the Hallowe'en party, but the girls had a few minutes free before it started. Paige was not looking forward to confronting the history teacher, but nobody had come up with a better idea than Shannon's so far, and Paige knew that they had to get the Eye of Heaven back.

Mrs Stockbridge was sorting through a pile of papers on her desk. She glanced up as the girls entered the room and smiled. It wasn't a nice smile, Paige thought. Mrs Stockbridge looked like the cat that got the cream. Paige wondered why they'd ever liked her.

"We want the Eye of Heaven back," Shannon said bluntly, coming to a stop in front of the teacher's desk. "It belongs at Charm Hall."

"And Estelle's journal too," Paige added.

"Oh, dear," Mrs Stockbridge said, smiling very smugly. "I'm afraid I have absolutely no idea what you're talking about, girls. All that research about Charm Hall, Estelle and the Eye of Heaven must have scrambled your brains."

"We know you've got it," Summer said quietly. "And it isn't yours. That makes you a thief!"

"Be careful, Summer," Mrs Stockbridge said, her voice steely. "You really shouldn't throw accusations like that around without proof." She narrowed her eyes. "And, anyway, even if I did have the sapphire, why on earth would I hand it over to you? It's extremely valuable, you know. My goodness, the person who owned it would be rich beyond their wildest dreams! They'd never have to work again!"

"But we *need* it here at Charm Hall!" Paige said

angrily. "Look at all the awful things that have happened today!"

Mrs Stockbridge laughed. "The idea that the sapphire is a charm is just a silly superstition," she declared, beginning to stack books in a cardboard box. "Now run along. I'm very busy with my packing. You see, I'm leaving Charm Hall tomorrow."

"Leaving?" Shannon gasped, glancing at Paige and Summer in shock.

Mrs Stockbridge smiled. "Yes, we're going to live abroad, somewhere very hot and *very* far away, but I shall be coming to the Hallowe'en party." Her smile grew wider. "What a wonderful send-off that will be! And now I must be getting home. I have to mark your Hallowe'en projects."

She picked up her box and strolled over to the door. "By the way," she said, pausing in the doorway, "let me congratulate you on your research, girls. It was very interesting and *very* useful! You'll get top marks for your project!" And, laughing triumphantly, Mrs Stockbridge sauntered off.

"We've got to get the sapphire away from her

before she leaves Charm Hall!" Shannon exclaimed. "Or we'll *never* get it back!"

"But what can we do?" wailed Summer.

"We'll think of something," said Paige as the assembly bell rang. "We're not giving up that easily!"

The girls hurried to join the rest of the school and arrived just before Miss Linnet.

"Before we discuss the party, I'm afraid I have some sad news, girls," the headteacher announced. "Unfortunately, Mrs Stockbridge has had a family emergency, and she is being forced to leave us at very short notice."

There was a murmur of surprise around the hall and many of the girls looked quite upset. *Mrs Stockbridge has been a popular teacher*, thought Paige. *But that's only because nobody knows what she's really like!*

"Now, I know that those of you who have been taught by Mrs Stockbridge will miss her greatly," Miss Linnet went on. "But you'll be pleased to hear that she'll be at the Hallowe'en party, and she'll also be coming trick or treating with us in the village beforehand. Speaking of which, you must be in your costumes and ready to leave by seven on Saturday evening. The minibus will be waiting for you . . ."

As Miss Linnet talked on about the arrangements for the party, an idea flashed into Paige's head. *If this plan works*, Paige thought with a thrill of excitement, *we might just be able to find the Eye of Heaven and bring it back to Charm Hall!*

Chapter Eleven

"I know how we might be able to get the sapphire back!" Paige told Shannon and Summer.

The girls were back in their dorm after assembly, making some decorations for the party. They'd spread some newspaper on the floor and were scooping out pumpkins to make lanterns. Velvet was perched on Shannon's bed, watching the proceedings with interest.

"How?" Shannon demanded eagerly, stopping halfway through scooping out her pumpkin.

Paige smiled. "I've been thinking this plan through since assembly. And now I really think it could work . . ."

"Tell us, Paige!" Summer urged.

"Well, we think the Eye of Heaven is in Mrs Stockbridge's house in the new village, right?" Paige began, sitting back on her heels as her friends nodded. "And tomorrow evening we're going trick or treating in the village. So all we have to do is hope that Mr Stockbridge is home, make up some excuse so that he lets us into the house, and then look for the sapphire!"

"Good thinking, Paige!" Shannon declared.

But Summer was frowning. "There are teachers going with us, though, and one of them is Mrs Stockbridge herself," she pointed out. "Don't you think someone might notice if we try to break away from the rest of the group?"

"I've thought of that," Paige sighed, glancing at her werewolf costume. It had taken her ages to sew on all that fake fur! 'You know how loads of girls are going as witches? Well—"

"If we go as witches too, we'll blend in with the crowd and then we'll be able to slip away to Mrs Stockbridge's house!" Summer finished for her. "That's brilliant!"

Shannon glanced sadly at the papier mâché

Frankenstein mask which lay on her desk. "I was really looking forward to wearing my mask!" she sighed. "But the sapphire's definitely more important. I suppose this means that we've got to make witches' costumes to wear on Saturday then?"

Paige nodded. "Let's get started," she said.

"Paige, your plan is working like a dream!" Summer whispered. "There are loads of witches here!"

It was Saturday evening, and Paige, Shannon and Summer were gathered with the rest of their year in the school entrance hall, ready to go trick or treating.

"There's no way we're going to win the prize for best costume," Shannon remarked, as Mrs Stockbridge and a couple of other teachers joined them. "There are just too many witches!"

"Never mind," said Paige. "We're looking for a much bigger prize – the Eye of Heaven!"

"Are we all ready?" Mrs Stockbridge enquired.

At that moment, Mia came rushing up to her. She, too, was dressed as a witch. Shannon and Summer both grinned at Paige.

"Abigail's not coming, miss," Mia said

breathlessly. "She's still working on her costume."

"Very well," Mrs Stockbridge said. "Come along then, girls. The minibus is waiting."

There was a real buzz in the air as everyone trooped out laughing and chatting. Paige, Summer and Shannon were last, and as they passed Mrs Stockbridge she gave them a glowing smile.

"You look fantastic as witches, girls!" she remarked. "Quite the little Estelle Charms, aren't you? In fact, I shall call you Estelle one, two and three from now on!"

Shannon looked like she was about to spit fire, and Paige hastily pulled her friend on to the minibus.

"We're going to find that sapphire if it's the last thing we do!" Shannon announced furiously, settling herself into a seat.

The bus pulled away down the school driveway, and came to a halt again by the village green.

"Now, have a good time, girls," said Mrs Stockbridge from the front of the bus, "but make sure you stay in groups of three or more. And don't go too far, please. I want you all back here in half an hour. We don't want to be late for the party, do we?"

110

Paige, Shannon and Summer tried to ignore Mrs Stockbridge and her self-satisfied smile as they climbed off the bus. The other girls were already spreading out in different directions, heading towards the houses. Meanwhile, the teachers walked up and down the street, keeping an eye on everyone.

"This way," Shannon whispered, pointing behind Mrs Stockbridge's back.

Quickly and quietly, the girls slipped away. Paige and Shannon remembered exactly where Mrs Stockbridge's house was, and as they hurried up the street towards it, Paige felt a flash of relief when she saw that the lights were on. If Mr Stockbridge had been out, their plan would have been ruined.

Shannon rang the bell and the girls waited on the doorstep. It seemed like ages before the door opened.

"Trick or treat!" the girls chorused.

Mr Stockbridge stood in the hall, looking a bit taken aback. Then he smiled. "Hello, you're the girls from my wife's school, aren't you?" he said, looking at Paige and Shannon. "I'm terribly sorry, but I don't have any sweets for you.' He looked rather embarrassed. "You see, we're moving away tomorrow and everything is boxed up, ready for the removal men."

"Oh, what a shame!" said Paige with a smile. "Don't worry, we won't play a trick on you, but do you think I could use your bathroom, please?"

To Paige's relief, Mr Stockbridge nodded.

"Come in," he said kindly. "It's upstairs on the left."

Paige, Summer and Shannon stepped into the hall and Paige shot upstairs as quickly as she could. Behind her she could hear Shannon and Summer talking to Mr Stockbridge.

Paige shut the bathroom door as noisily as she could, and then tiptoed along the landing. There were three bedrooms full of boxes which had been packed ready for the move, and Paige had to squeeze her way around them. The boxes were taped firmly shut, but Paige had a feeling that Mrs Stockbridge wouldn't have packed the jewel away in one of them. After all, the boxes would be taken away by the removal men, and Paige was sure that Mrs Stockbridge would want the Eye of Heaven to travel with her.

Paige hurried from room to room, searching every cupboard and shelf that caught her eye, but she found nothing. Finally, she slipped into the smallest bedroom and looked around, but the Eye of Heaven didn't seem to be there either.

Paige was just wondering what she should do next, when to her horror, she heard Mr Stockbridge coming up the stairs.

Chapter Twelve

Paige just had time to run out on to the landing and over to the top of the staircase.

Two seconds later Mr Stockbridge came round the curve of the stairs. "Ah, there you are," he said with a smile. "I thought you might have got lost!"

"No, I'm fine, thanks," Paige said brightly, even though inside she felt miserable that she hadn't found the Eye of Heaven. She had no choice but to follow Mr Stockbridge back downstairs.

Summer and Shannon were standing in the hall staring hopefully up at Paige as she came down. Suddenly, there was the sound of a key in the lock and the front door swung open. Mrs Stockbridge walked in.

The teacher stopped dead when she saw the three girls, the colour draining from her face.

"Wh-what are *you* doing here?" she stammered.

"That's obvious, isn't it, Susan?" Mr Stockbridge said jokingly. "They're trick or treating!"

Mrs Stockbridge was looking very flustered, and Paige guessed that her husband knew nothing about her theft of the sapphire. "Yes, well, they were told not to go too far from the bus!" she snapped.

Another idea suddenly flashed into Paige's head. "Sorry, Mrs Stockbridge," she said cheerfully. "We got a bit carried away."

"You three go back to the minibus," Mrs Stockbridge said coldly. "I've just popped home to change my coat; it's colder than I thought."

"OK, we'll see you back there," Paige replied. Then, as she walked past Mrs Stockbridge towards the front door, she added, in a low voice, "We've found what we were looking for, anyway!"

Mrs Stockbridge's face was a picture of fury as Paige, Shannon and Summer left the house.

"You found it!" Summer gasped, her eyes shining.

Shannon patted Paige on the back. "Brilliant!" she laughed.

"I *didn't* find it," Paige told them sadly. "But I wanted Mrs S to *think* that I had."

Summer and Shannon stared at her blankly.

"I'm hoping that the first thing Mrs Stockbridge will do now is go and check that the sapphire's still where she hid it!" Paige explained quickly. "If we watch through the windows and see which room she goes into, we might discover her hiding place – but we'll have to be quick about it!"

"I'll take the front," Shannon said, hurrying behind a large bush in front of the living room window.

Summer and Paige dashed round into the back garden.

"We can't cover *every* window," Summer pointed out as she peered into the kitchen. "We can't see upstairs."

"Maybe we can, though . . ." Paige said slowly, pointing at a large apple tree next to the house. One of the branches reached out towards one of the upper windows. "You stay here, Summer. I'll look upstairs."

116

Paige climbed up the tree, being careful not to catch her long black dress. She lay down along the branch that stretched towards the bedroom window and peeped into the house. The room was in darkness.

Suddenly the light was switched on. Paige ducked as low as she could so that she wouldn't be seen. At the same moment she thought she saw a black shadow streak across the room. But she didn't have time to think about that because she saw Mrs Stockbridge standing in the doorway.

Paige watched, hardly daring to breathe, as the teacher rushed in and prised up one of the floorboards. She peered down into the gap in the floor and then nodded, smiling with relief.

Paige felt her heart begin to pound with excitement as Mrs Stockbridge left the room again, switching the light off but leaving the door slightly ajar.

"Summer!" Paige called softly. "Fetch Shannon and climb up here with me. I know where the Eye of Heaven is!"

Paige watched as Summer disappeared round the side of the house. Moments later she was back with

Shannon, and the two of them quickly scrambled up to join Paige in the apple tree.

"Where is it, Paige?" whispered Shannon eagerly.

"It's under a floorboard in the middle of the room," Paige explained, pointing through the window. "Somehow we have to try and get into that bedroom!"

Suddenly, Shannon let out a gasp. "Look!" she whispered, pointing at the window.

Paige turned and saw a pair of amber eyes staring back at her from inside the room. "Oh!" Paige whispered excitedly. "It's Velvet!"

Chapter Thirteen

"She's come to help us get the Eye of Heaven back!" Shannon exclaimed.

Velvet was staring steadily at the girls. Then Paige felt a rush of excitement as she saw Velvet's whiskers start to shimmer with the golden gleam of magic.

"Look at the window!" Summer whispered.

Paige stared in amazement. The window had begun to ripple and pulse as if it were made of water rather than solid glass.

Cautiously, Paige put out her hand and touched the glass. It wobbled underneath her fingers, like jelly. Paige pushed harder and her fingers went right through the window and into the bedroom on the other side. Curiously, Summer did the same, pushing her whole arm through. Velvet trilled with pleasure and jumped down from the window sill. Then she sat on the floor, looking up at the girls expectantly.

"Let's go for it!" said Shannon. Quickly she squashed an arm, then a leg, and then the whole of her body through the window.

A few seconds later she was waving at Summer and Paige from inside the bedroom.

Quickly, Paige and Summer followed. *It's like squeezing through a huge bowl of jelly*, Paige thought, as she made it safely to the other side.

"Now, where's the loose floorboard, Paige?" Shannon asked quietly.

"Over here," Paige replied, heading over to the right one.

She saw that the floorboard had a small hole in one end. Quickly she hooked her little finger into the hole and pulled the floorboard up.

Underneath, in the floor cavity, sat Estelle Charm's journal, and on top of it was a bundle wrapped in tissue paper.

Paige picked it up and unwrapped it. "Oh!" she breathed. "It's beautiful!"

The gold necklace they had seen on the computer lay on Paige's palm, and, in the centre, the Eye of Heaven flashed a deep, deep blue in the moonlight. For a second all three girls were mesmerized by its beauty.

"We'd better get out of here," Shannon urged.

Paige wrapped the necklace up again and put it

121

safely in her pocket. Summer tucked Estelle's journal under her arm, covering it with her black witch's cape, and then the three girls hurried over to the window. They squeezed themselves back through the jelly glass to the other side and climbed back into the apple tree.

"Come on, Velvet!" Paige whispered, turning back to the window.

But the window was now solid glass again, and Velvet was nowhere to be seen.

"She's probably back home already," Shannon said as they climbed down. "And, thanks to her, we've got the Eye of Heaven back!"

"We'd better get back to the minibus," Summer whispered as they tiptoed out of the Stockbridges' garden. "It's almost time for the party to start."

"And I'm *really* going to enjoy it now that we have the Eye of Heaven back!" Paige added happily.

Everyone was already climbing on to the bus as Paige, Shannon and Summer joined the group. Mrs Stockbridge smiled and waved merrily at them as they too boarded the bus.

"She thinks the sapphire's still safe under her

floorboards!" Shannon whispered. "How wrong is she?"

"Don't smile!" Summer hissed. "Look miserable. We don't want her to guess that we've got it!"

When the minibus arrived back at the school, the party was just getting underway. The girls popped upstairs to hide Estelle's journal, and found Velvet curled up happily on Shannon's bed.

"I told you she'd be home before us!" Shannon laughed.

All three girls stopped to make a fuss of the magical kitten and then they hurried downstairs to join the party.

The assembly hall had been transformed with lots of white tissue-paper ghosts and black cardboard bats bobbing around on elastic strings. A pumpkin lantern sat in the middle of every table, and some of the girls were dancing to the music blaring from the sound system. A couple of teachers were setting up some Hallowe'en games, like apple bobbing and pin-the-bone-on-the-skeleton.

Suddenly, a burst of loud laughter behind them made the girls turn. Paige glanced round to see a big orange pumpkin waddling towards them.

Shannon clutched Paige's arm. "Is that . . . is that *Abigail?*" she stammered.

Paige nodded, unable to tear her eyes away from the orange vision in front of her. Abigail was almost completely swamped by an enormous pumpkin costume. Paige was surprised that Abigail had actually managed to fit through the hall doors.

The pumpkin was made of lots of strips of orange material which had been sewn together, and then padded out to make it round and fat. Abigail's head poked out of a hole in the top. She wore a little felt necklace of green leaves, and her face was painted green too. Paige couldn't help giggling. It was a ridiculous sight, but it was also an impressive costume. Abigail must have spent ages constructing it.

Shannon and Summer were laughing too, along with everyone else in the hall.

"I wish I had my camera with me!" Paige murmured as Abigail waddled over, with Mia running along behind her.

"That's quite a costume, Abigail," Shannon remarked, trying to keep a straight face.

Abigail looked at Shannon and then frowned.

"I thought you three were coming as pumpkins!" she snapped.

"No," Summer replied, puzzled. "Why would you think that?"

Abigail looked a bit sheepish. "Oh, er . . . no reason . . ." she mumbled.

Mia frowned. "I thought you said you'd overheard Shannon going on about pumpkins being a winner at Hallowe'en?" she said.

"Oh, yes," Paige murmured, suddenly remembering the day they had had lunch out on the terrace, when Abigail had come up behind them and taken their table.

"Aha!" Shannon exclaimed, raising her eyebrows at Abigail. "You thought I meant that we were going to dress up as pumpkins!" She shook her head. "I was talking about the Hallowe'en decorations, not our *costumes*!"

"Oh . . ." Abigail looked completely deflated, and Paige guessed that she had been trying to ensure her pumpkin costume was more impressive than theirs.

"Abigail?" Chloe appeared at her side. "It's our turn to bob for apples. I've been looking for you."

"Well, I'm not hard to spot!" Abigail snapped. "After all, I *am* bright orange!"

Paige tried not to laugh.

"It's all been a waste of time, Mia," Abigail moaned as she stalked off. "All those late nights and early mornings we spent sewing this costume together, and those three have come as witches! And now everyone's laughing at me because pumpkins aren't at all glamorous . . ."

"I feel a bit sorry for Abigail," Paige admitted.

"And Mia, too. It sounds like she got roped in to help!"

"It *is* a pretty impressive costume, though," Summer remarked.

"And now we know why Abigail was spying on us all the time," Paige pointed out. "She wanted to find out what we were wearing after Shannon made that comment about how brilliant our costumes were going to be!"

"Well, that's one mystery solved. Now let's have something to eat," said Summer. "We should be celebrating now that we've got the Eye of Heaven back!"

"OK, but after seeing Abigail, I don't think I fancy any of the pumpkin pie!" Shannon said with a grin.

The party has been fantastic! Paige thought happily a couple of hours later, as she and Summer watched a blindfolded Shannon trying to pin the bone on the skeleton. *Especially because I've got the Eye of Heaven safe and sound in my pocket.*

At the end of the evening, Miss Linnet went on stage to announce the winner of the best costume prize. "Well, girls, you've all worked very hard to make the party a big success," she said with a smile. "And we've seen some wonderful costumes. But the prize of two cinema tickets goes to the biggest pumpkin I have ever seen – Abigail Carter!"

There was a burst of applause as Abigail waddled over to the stage and Miss Linnet presented her with her prize.

"I won!" Abigail cried triumphantly, throwing Shannon a gleeful look before waddling off the stage. "You can come to the cinema with me, Mia. After all, you did help me a tiny bit!"

Paige grinned at the look on Mia's face.

"Typical Abigail!" Shannon chuckled. "I bet she had Mia working all hours, but she still takes all the credit!"

The party began to wind down after that, and the three friends eventually headed upstairs to their dorm. Paige felt tired but extremely happy. *Tomorrow Mrs Stockbridge will be jetting off somewhere far, far away* without *the Eye of Heaven*, she thought. *There's just one more thing that we need to do . . .*

"You know, we have to find a new hiding place for the sapphire," she pointed out. "Somewhere that

Mrs Stockbridge won't be able to find it, even if she *does* come back to Charm Hall."

The others nodded.

"Look," Shannon said. "There's Velvet!"

The little black kitten was perched on one of the gargoyles which lined the stairs. She sprang to her feet as the girls approached, balancing neatly on the gargoyle's head, which was large and round with very big ears. Then she mewed loudly at the girls.

"Thanks for everything, Velvet!" Paige said, smiling at the kitten.

"You're such a clever girl," Summer said, stroking her lovingly. "But now it's bedtime for all of us."

"Look, her whiskers are glowing!" Shannon exclaimed. "And her tail's flicking from side to side! You know what that means . . ."

Suddenly, with a soft creak, the gargoyle's ear twisted to one side.

"What's—" Paige began, but she didn't have time to say anything more, because the stair she was standing on was sliding sideways under her feet.

Chapter Fourteen

Shannon and Summer, who were standing on the stair above, laughed as Paige hurriedly jumped off the step and on to the one below. Then they all knelt down to peer into the gap left by the sliding stair.

"It's a secret compartment!" Shannon announced.

"I think Velvet's just shown us the sapphire's new hiding place," Summer said with a grin.

Paige took the necklace from her pocket and unwrapped it quickly for one last look. The girls stared at the beautiful sapphire in silence for a few seconds, and then Paige placed it gently in the

secret compartment. Velvet immediately jumped down from the gargoyle and the stair slid smoothly back into place.

Paige peered closely at it. It looked exactly the same as all the other stairs now.

"Mission accomplished!" Shannon yawned as Velvet trotted off ahead of them. "Let's get to bed!"

What a brilliant day! Paige thought sleepily to herself, as she snuggled down under her duvet and listened to Velvet's rhythmic purring coming from the end of her bed. *We got the sapphire back, the party was great – and Mrs Stockbridge is in for a big surprise!*

"Did you enjoy the party, girls?" asked Joan as she gave Shannon a generous helping of scrambled eggs the following morning.

"Fantastic, thanks!" Shannon replied cheerfully. "And the food was great! How's your car?"

"It's all fixed now," Joan said happily. "But, when I was driving here this morning, a big branch fell off a tree and nearly hit me!"

"It *nearly* hit you?" Paige repeated.

Joan nodded. "Yes, it just missed my car by a whisker!" she replied. "I was lucky, because it might have caused a lot of damage!"

"The Eye of Heaven is protecting Charm Hall again!" Summer whispered to Paige and Shannon as they went to find a table. "Isn't that great?"

Paige and Shannon nodded happily.

As it was Sunday, the girls spent a lazy morning

reading and playing board games.

"I wonder if Mrs Stockbridge has left yet," Paige said as they went to the dining hall for lunch later that day.

"I haven't seen her in school so maybe she has," Shannon replied. "Good riddance!"

But just then, Mrs Stockbridge appeared around the corner in front of them. Paige felt her heart begin to hammer as the teacher stopped, blocking their path. Mrs Stockbridge looked angry and frustrated. She'd obviously found out that the sapphire was not where she'd left it.

"Where's the Eye of Heaven?" she demanded furiously.

Paige smiled. "We have absolutely no idea what you're talking about, Mrs Stockbridge," she said, echoing the teacher's own words when they'd asked her to give the jewel back.

"And even if we *did* have the sapphire," Summer added, "why would we tell you?"

"The Eye of Heaven is right where it belongs!" Shannon said firmly.

Mrs Stockbridge's eyes narrowed and she took a step towards the girls.

"Ah, I see you're saying your goodbyes to Mrs Stockbridge," Miss Linnet said, coming along the corridor at that moment. "I'm sure Mrs Stockbridge is going to miss teaching you. She tells me your project was excellent!"

"Yes, Miss Linnet, they're quite the most resourceful pupils I've ever had the privilege of teaching!" Mrs Stockbridge said, with a smile that didn't reach her eyes. "Goodbye.' She nodded at Miss Linnet and strode off down the corridor.

"Don't be too sad, girls," said the headteacher comfortingly. "It's always sad to say goodbye to an unforgettable teacher like Mrs Stockbridge."

Paige tried not to smile as she glanced at her friends. Mrs Stockbridge certainly was unforgettable, but, thanks to Velvet, she was leaving Charm Hall *without* the precious Eye of Heaven. *Which, Paige thought, is just what Estelle Charm would have wanted!*

If you want to read more

about the **magic** at

Charm Hall, then

turn over for the start of

the neXt adventure ...

Charm Hall

Mona Lisa
Mystery

Chapter One

Paige Hart opened her eyes. She was suddenly wide awake. A familiar sound had woken her up, but she couldn't quite remember what it was. It was dark in the attic dormitory, with just a slice of silver moonlight shining through a crack in the curtains. Paige lay there listening to the soft, slow breathing of her dorm-mates, Shannon and Summer, then wriggled into a more comfortable position. Maybe she'd dreamed that she'd heard something.

But then, suddenly, the sound came again. *Miaow!* It was Velvet, the little black kitten who was the girls' secret pet.

Paige sat up and stared around in the darkness. There, on Paige's bedside table, sat Velvet, her golden eyes glowing in the dark. Paige glanced at her alarm clock. It was five minutes to midnight.

"What's up, puss?" she asked Velvet, reaching out to stroke her, but Velvet immediately jumped down from the bedside table and ran swiftly across the room.

Paige watched as Velvet trotted over to Shannon's bed, miaowed loudly, and then used a paw to tap one of Shannon's hands that was dangling over the side of the bed.

Shannon stirred. "Velvet?" she murmured groggily, sitting up. "What's wrong?"

But Velvet was already padding across the carpet to Summer's bed, where she leaped lightly on to the pillow and rubbed her head against Summer's cheek.

Paige was feeling more awake by the second. Velvet was acting very strangely. "Velvet, what is it?" she asked, swinging her legs out of bed and pulling on her dressing gown with a shiver. It was cold and she could hear the wind gusting around the rooftops outside. She flicked on her lamp to see that Velvet was now scrabbling at the door.

"She wants to show us something," Shannon said, now wide awake too. "She's never woken us up like this before, has she?"

"And it's not like she needs *our* help to get in and out of the room," Summer agreed, pushing her bare feet into slippers.

Velvet had come in through the window one day, not long after Paige had started at Charm Hall Boarding School, and Paige and her friends had quickly realized that Velvet was no ordinary black kitten – she had special magical powers!

"So, what are we waiting for?" Shannon asked, grabbing the torch from the drawer of her bedside table. "Let's go!"

Paige felt prickly with excitement. "We'll have to be really quiet," she whispered. "If we get caught, we'll be in big trouble!"

Velvet mewed, as if in agreement, and Summer opened the bedroom door.

Shannon turned on her torch and Velvet led the way, her paws silent on the wooden staircases and along the hallways. To Paige's mind, Velvet looked like an inky shadow, slipping along the corridor. The girls tiptoed after her, through the school, until they reached the back door.

Velvet stood on her hind legs and scratched at the door. The girls exchanged glances.

"You want us to go *outside?*" Summer asked. "In the middle of the night?"

Velvet miaowed loudly.

"I think that was a 'yes'," Paige said. "Come on." She turned the door handle and pushed – but the door stayed firmly shut. "Oh, it's locked!" she whispered disappointedly.

"And it's bolted at the top," Shannon added, shining her torch up to show the others. "How are we going to get out?"

Velvet sat down, whisking her tail from side to side behind her. Her whiskers began to shimmer with a bright golden gleam, and Paige felt a thrill of excitement. She'd seen Velvet's magic many times now, but she still couldn't help being completely mesmerized by it.

A stream of golden sparkles swirled up around Velvet's body, and then zoomed over to the door, fizzing and sparkling like tiny fireflies. The next moment, the bolt slid back silently, and the girls heard the lock clicking open.

Paige tried the door handle again and this time the door swung open easily. "Nice one, Velvet!" she said with a grin, stepping through the doorway. Outside, the frosty ground sparkled silver in the moonlight. "Wow, it's like being in a Christmas card," Paige breathed.

A cold wind snaked around Paige's ankles, and she shivered.

"Brrr," Shannon said, rubbing her arms. "We must be mad, being out in the middle of the night in November!"

Before anyone could reply, Paige heard the faint sound of sobbing, carried on the wind. "Who's that?" she hissed.

Shannon and Summer listened hard. "Well, whoever it is, they're crying their heart out," Summer replied. "Is that why you brought us out here, Velvet? Is someone in trouble?"

Velvet was already picking her way across the terrace, towards the sound of the crying, her tail swaying in the air. The frost crunched under the girls' feet as they followed the little kitten.

Velvet led them to a large, old oak tree and
Paige's eyes widened when she saw a little girl
crouched at the foot of the tree in the darkness.
The girl was sobbing with her head on her knees,
but Paige was certain she wasn't a Charm Hall
student – she was too young. Paige thought she
could only be about five or six years old. So who
was she, and where had she come from?

Paige, Summer and Shannon ran over to her.

"Hello," Paige said, kneeling down beside the little girl. "What's wrong?"

The little girl didn't reply.

Summer and Shannon crouched down next to Paige. "What are you doing out here?" Summer asked the little girl gently.

The little girl looked up, her dark eyes swollen from crying. "I was trying to run away," she said mournfully.

Velvet walked over and pushed her little black head against the girl's hand. The girl gave a surprised smile as she saw Velvet. "Hello, kitty," she said, stroking Velvet, who immediately let out a rumbling purr.

Shannon put her arm around the little girl. "I'm Shannon," she said. "And this is Velvet. What's your name? And why were you trying to run away?"

"I'm Lily," the little girl replied, wiping her tears away with the back of one hand. Velvet clambered into her lap, still purring, and Lily stroked her. "I'm staying with my Grandpa Sam," she went on. "He works at the school. But I don't want to live here. I want to go home to my mum and dad!"

Something clicked in Paige's head. "Sam – do you mean the caretaker?" she asked. "He has a cottage around here, doesn't he?"

Lily nodded. "Yes," she said, staring down at Velvet. "Mum and Dad say I have to stay with him while they . . . 'sort things out'." She bit her lip. "They've been arguing a lot, and Dad went away for a few days. Then he came back, and . . ." she sighed, "they said I had to come here. But I want to go home. I miss them – and my friends too."

"That sounds rough," Summer said sympathetically. "But you shouldn't be out here in the cold."

"Your grandpa will be dead worried if he finds you've gone," Shannon added. "We'd better take you back to his house. Hopefully your mum and dad will soon sort things out." Shannon got to her feet and held out a hand to Lily.

Velvet jumped off Lily's lap, and the young girl got to her feet. "I didn't mean to make Grandpa Sam upset," she said. "I just . . ."

"Don't worry," Paige assured her. "He'll just be glad to have you back safe and sound. Now, let's go. It's freezing!"

With magic in the air at Charm Hall, this is one boarding school where anything can happen!

Paige can't believe she didn't want to come
to Charm Hall now that she's met Summer
and Shannon, her new best friends.

Then a black kitten mysteriously appears.
She's so cute they don't have the heart to
get rid of her, especially when she turns out
to be more than just an average kitten!

Hodder
Children's
Books

A division of Hachette Children's Books

With magic in the air at Charm Hall, this is one boarding school where anything can happen!

Paige and Shannon think Summer would be
brilliant as Puck in the school's play of
A Midsummer Night's Dream, but she's so shy.
Luckily Velvet, their secret pet kitten,
has a plan that will change all that.

But someone is out to sabotage the play
and the girls are determined to find
out who the culprit is.

h
Hodder
Children's
Books

A division of Hachette Children's Books

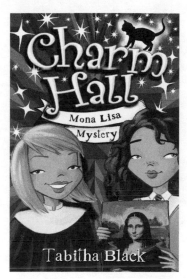

Charm Hall
Mona Lisa Mystery
Tabitha Black

With magic in the air at Charm Hall, this is one boarding school where anything can happen!

It's Christmas time and the choir enter a carol competition. But then they find out another school is singing the same carols!

Velvet takes Paige, Summer and Shannon back in time to solve the mystery of why the famous Mona Lisa is smiling and they find a way to save the choir, too.

A division of Hachette Children's Books

Charm Hall
A Note of Danger

With magic in the air at Charm Hall,
this is one boarding school where
anything can happen!

Paige, Summer and Shannon are all excited
about sports day but Shannon isn't sure she
can win against Abigail. That is until Velvet
finds a way to boost her confidence.

But then the girls discover someone
who needs help even more –
a friend who's being blackmailed!

Hodder
Children's
Books

A division of Hachette Children's Books

Mirror Magic

With magic in the air at Charm Hall,
this is one boarding school where
anything can happen!

Paige, Summer and Shannon can't believe
Marmalade, the world famous popstar,
is going to perform at Charm Hall.

With Velvet, they find a way to see the future -
but when they discover a kidnap plot,
they're not sure if they can stop it in time!

h
Hodder
Children's
Books

A division of Hachette Children's Books